PLANET XANADU

PLANET XANADU

LAMEES ALHASSAR

Lamees LLC

Copyright © 2021 by Lamees Alhassar

All rights reserved. No part of this book may be reproduced in any manner whatsoever without written permission except in the case of brief quotations embodied in critical articles and reviews.

First Printing, 2021

To all my fans...Thank you.

CHAPTER 1

"How can we be invaded?"

Rather than a response, all she heard was silence.

President Jane Parker was standing at the head of a large mahogany table. Seated around it were several men and women dressed in black and blue suits.

"Am I not talking to my trusted advisors? Or is the 97th President of the United States simply talking to herself?" she asked.

She saw one of the men raise his hand. "Yes, Defense Secretary, what do you have to say?"

"Madam President, I don't mean to be blunt, but the answer to your question is 'yes'. Yes, Earth is about to be invaded and there is nothing that we can do about it."

"I admire how blunt you are, Mr. Secretary. But with such a response, you might as well have also handed over your resignation letter to this Council. Do you realize what you've just said?"

The Defense Secretary raised his hand again, but the President didn't allow him to speak. Rather, she continued with what she was saying. "Your statement is an outright admission of your incompetence. What do you expect our nation to do? Sit on our chairs and twiddle our thumbs, waiting for the planet to be taken over? Because that's what you are implying."

He raised his hand yet again, but the President still didn't let him talk. "You do realize that other countries still look up to the United States, don't you? And do you know why? It's because we are a beacon of hope, strength, and security. What do you expect me to tell them? That we are helpless?"

The Secretary of Defense dropped his hand and sighed. He clenched his fists before slamming them hard on the table as he abruptly stood up, "Madam President. You need to come to terms with what I've just said. Yes, yes, and yes again. We can't do anything about the impending invasion. And if you want to know what you should tell the world, then I'm going to tell you. Just tell them the truth."

President Parker sighed and sat down slowly. "The truth? What is the truth?"

The Defense Secretary looked at the other men and women seated around the table. "Is there anything that we don't know yet? This Council has been privileged enough to follow all the developments and incidents that led us to where we are today. There's nothing hidden from any one of us."

A woman raised her hand. President Parker looked at her. "Yes, Science Secretary, you may speak."

"I think that my counterpart may have confused matters. What invasion is he talking about? As far as I'm concerned, all that we have right now are stationary UFOs, not an invasion by unknown or hostile entities."

The Defense Secretary frowned. "How can you make such an irresponsible statement? Are you trying to tell me that you can't recognize what an impending invasion looks like?"

"Mr. Defense Secretary, may I remind you that the members of this Council believe in working with facts and figures? For now, we have not yet seen any proof that Earth is about to be invaded. Rather, the truth of the matter is that we are being visited. And I must emphasize that it is a visit by unknown entities, not an invasion as you would like us to believe."

The Defense Secretary was about to argue further with the Science Secretary when the President raised her hand. "Enough, Mr. Defense Secretary."

The Defense Secretary shook his head and sat down quietly.

The President pointed at the Science Secretary. "There seems to be some hope in what you've just told us. I'm sure that after we've been brutalized by the doomsday prophesies of our dear colleague, we, the members of this Council, would like to hear what you have to say."

The Science Secretary stood up. "Madam President, we must look at the events in their proper perspective. In order to do so, we must take another look at the live feed that NASA has been monitoring since yesterday."

As she said this, she picked up a remote control close to her tablet and pointed it at the large screen on the wall. "As you can see from this image, nothing could be further from the truth about our dear planet being visited."

The men and women in the room turned their attention to the screen. It depicted a huge ball of green, blue, and brown floating in the black void of space. Earth was still a splendid feat of nature to look at from any distance. Around it, some satellites could be seen, revolving ever so slowly. Some distance away from the farthest and most visible satellite were thousands of alien spacecrafts of different shapes and sizes.

The spacecrafts were floating in space and maintained a semi-circular formation, but remained pointed towards Earth. The spacecrafts' bodies were reflective, which caused light from the sun to deflect off their smooth, silver surfaces.

"Madam President," the Science Secretary continued, "my fellow distinguished colleagues, this is a live feed from one of our satellites at the edge of Earth's atmosphere. These images are being closely monitored by NASA and other space agencies around the world. Those spaceships have been in that same position for the past twenty-four hours. Tell me, what do you really see?"

There was a hesitant murmur among those seated in the room.

The Science Secretary nodded as she looked around at her colleagues. "Exactly. Your guess is as good as mine. Even though they have made no contact with us, they don't look like a fleet about to launch an invasion upon our dear planet. Rather, from what NASA and other space agencies have been able to deduce, the spacecrafts seem to be conferring between themselves about how to approach us."

The Defense Secretary stood up. "Conferring amongst themselves? Would they really be discussing how to approach us, or are they deciding how to attack us? Please, people, can't you see what is about to happen?"

The President looked at the Defense Secretary. "I don't see anything about to happen, Mr. Defense Secretary. Or is there something else that these clear images are showing that I can't see?"

The Defense Secretary turned to the President. "Madam President, let's forget about what's happening presently and come back down to our level here on Earth. Imagine, for instance, that you plan on paying a visit to the Russians, or the Chinese, or maybe the Koreans. Would you march to their border with your entire entourage, then start a meeting with your staff in the same way that these strangers are doing in the sky?"

The President looked back at the screen and shook her head. "Well, not exactly."

"That's my point, Madam President. Whatever deliberations need to be made are completed long before you decide to embark on your trip. And even then, if you have an urgent need to confer with your entourage, which may of course happen, you would never do it in full view of your intended hosts. No, Madam President, I refuse to agree with the Science Secretary. This is a clear act of provocation, and the sooner we take counter-offensive measures, the better it will be for everyone on this planet."

"But why should we take any counter-offensive measures when they haven't given us any reason to do so?" the President asked.

"Reason? Are you waiting for a reason before protecting yourself? Fine, how about the fact that every attempt any government has made to communicate with them so far has been rebuffed?"

The President frowned. "Rebuffed?" She turned to the Science Secretary. "Is that true? Have we already made attempts to communicate with these alien visitors?"

The Science Secretary nodded. "Yes, Madam President. We've been trying to get in touch with them. But, unlike what the Defense Secretary has just said, I refuse to agree that we are being rebuffed. In fact, I believe we haven't been able to determine the right code, frequency or channel to establish communication."

The Defense Secretary shook his head. "I don't believe this. The right frequency or channel? Are you serious?"

"Of course I'm serious. If we go back to your example—assuming you wanted to communicate with a government you were visiting, wouldn't you want the appropriate language to do so? And where there is no common language, the next best bet is to find a way of translating their language into one that you understand, correct? That's the common standard in international relations, at least on Earth."

"So what is it now?" the Defense Secretary asked. "Are you trying to develop a translation method already?"

The Science Secretary nodded. "Yes, of course."

"You just said that they haven't been responding to our attempts to contact them!" the Defense Secretary scoffed. "How do you translate a language that you haven't heard and have no record or concept of?"

"Alright, that's enough you two," the President said. "If I must remind you all, the point of this Council meeting is to adopt a position which will be presented to the United Nations Security Council. As a chairperson of the Council, I can't tell them that the world should simply give in and expect an invasion, as the Defense Secretary has suggested. And if we decide to treat these unknown and unidentified beings as visitors, what should our approach be? And how do we handle them?"

Another man raised his hand. The President nodded at him. "Yes, International Affairs Secretary? Would you like to make a contribution?"

"Yes, Madam President. I was wondering if the Science Secretary could be more explicit about the progress that's been made in regards to communicating with the visitors."

The Science Secretary pointed at the screen. "Well, like I said, we really haven't made much headway. If we had, I doubt if our guests would still be waiting where they are right now. Who knows, perhaps they'd be guests at the White House already!"

"So, in other words, we've tried but still haven't gotten through to them?" the International Affairs Secretary asked.

The Science Secretary nodded. "Yes, but just for now. We believe we should be able to make a breakthrough soon."

"Why don't we simply approach them?" the International Affairs Secretary asked.

The Science Secretary stared at him with her mouth wide open. "What?"

The International Affairs Secretary nodded. "Yes, we should go to them directly, rather than waiting for them to respond to our various messages. If we were to get physically close enough to them, I'm sure that they would want to respond to our physical presence much more than they would want to respond to our messages."

The President frowned. "You think that approach would work?"

"Yes, Madam President. It should work. If you ask me, we've just been wasting time trying to communicate with these visitors in a code or language that might not be comprehensible to them. But if we were to physically approach them in a peaceful manner, they would be forced to reciprocate. By so doing, they would definitely have no choice other than to welcome us and open up or develop a way to communicate," the International Affairs Secretary said.

The Defense Secretary shook his head. "This is madness and suicide all mixed together in one big pot. Madam President, please, no matter what you do, don't listen to any of this. We should adopt a more severe approach. Have you thought about the possibility that all this is just a ploy by the so-called 'visitors' to access our defense systems before an invasion?"

"And have you thought about considering what both your Science and International Affairs counterparts have been trying to say all this time? Have you thought of the fact that maybe, just maybe, this time you might be wrong?"

"But what if I'm right, Madam President?" the Defense Secretary asked. "What if we *do* get invaded?"

The President shook her head. "Then we know we were wrong in our initial assessment of the present situation."

The Defense Secretary sighed. He then wiped his forehead with the back of his hand. "Look, maybe we can simply make an adjustment to my colleague's crazy idea here."

"What sort of adjustment?" the International Affairs Secretary asked.

"You really think that we should make physical contact and approach these beings or things or whatever it is that they are, right?" the Defense Secretary asked.

The International Affairs Secretary nodded. "Yes. We should send some of our people out there to see them, meet with them, and try to engage with them peacefully."

"I see. Then why don't we do so, but with a contingency plan in place?"

"A contingency plan?" the President asked.

The Defense Secretary nodded. "Yes, Madam President. A contingency plan in which our forces would be on stand-by for any unforeseen eventuality. We really don't know who they are or what they want. It would be completely suicidal to send our people out there and hope that nothing unexpected might happen."

The President turned to her International Affairs Secretary. "What do you think?"

"Well, at least it's not what he was suggesting initially, adopting an aggressive response towards them straight off. The point is that we should go out there to meet them. Anything else that we do back on Earth to protect ourselves from any unexpected eventuality should be alright."

"Right, I think we have a plan then," the President nodded. "The US will vote for Earth to pay a visit to our unknown guests while ensuring that our defense systems are on high alert. It will be the responsibility of the UN Security Council to select the team. Frankly, this should be a winner at the UN. For once, let us have a mindset of peace instead of conflict or conflict resolution."

After the Council meeting adjourned, the President walked out of the room into the courtyard. She was accompanied by her Vice President, the Secretary of State, and some of her security detail.

They all boarded the helicopter that had been waiting outside. Before long, they had disappeared over the horizon.

CHAPTER 2

The helicopter landed on a helipad atop the white and grey headquarters of the United Nations.

As President Parker walked into one of the meeting rooms, the doors were shut behind her by the security orderlies. Inside, she greeted the other four delegates who were waiting for her.

"What's this we're hearing?" asked a delegate, as President Parker sat down.

"Hello, Russia. What have you heard?" President Parker responded.

The Russian President looked at the others seated at the table. "I hope you are aware that in my country, we've been closely monitoring the unfolding developments outside the Earth's atmosphere. I'm very sure that you all have been doing so as well."

The other three delegates, one woman and two men, nodded in unison.

"We have, Mr. President. Before I left Beijing for this meeting, we thought it would be necessary to adopt a stringent approach to handling these invaders," the Chinese President said.

"A stringent approach?" President Parker asked. "And what might that be?"

"We need to activate our attack protocols, of course," the Chinese President replied.

"Is that so? And who else favors such an approach?" President Parker asked.

The Russian and Chinese presidents raised their hands.

"I can see only two of you. Well, it might interest you to know that the United States thinks otherwise. We want to assume that these are visitors to our planet and not invaders."

The Russian President shook his head. "That's a grave error, Madam President. Have you noticed how close they are to our planet and how long they've been there? That seems to be more of a provocation to me, rather than a visitation."

"Well, if you don't favor an aggressive response, what do you have in mind?" the Chinese President asked.

"My country is suggesting that we pay these beings a visit ourselves," President Parker replied.

"A visit?" the Chinese President asked.

"Yes, and to ensure that we're not caught off-guard, we'd keep all our defense systems on high alert, in case any unforeseen situations arise."

"Unforeseen situations? Come on, Madam President. We already know what will happen. Those beings are hostile; they're going to strike us down at the first opportunity they get, and sending anyone up there to pay them a visit is simply out of the question. No, my country will not support such a reckless move."

The Chinese President frowned. "Yes, I agree with my Russian counterpart. President Parker, you should know better than to think of such a move. We should be preparing for an aggressive response, not thinking of organizing a welcome party."

"Well, that's the beauty of democracy, isn't it?" President Parker said.

The other two delegates—the French President and the UK Prime Minister—glanced at each other and shook their heads. But before either of them could offer a response, they all felt a slight tremor. It was subtle but noticeable enough for President Parker to frown and look around the room.

"What was that?" the Chinese President asked.

"I was just about to ask the same thing," the Russian President added, looking around the room. "President Parker, I thought New York City wasn't prone to such tremors and earthquakes!"

"I don't doubt how accurate and in-depth your knowledge of earthquakes in my country is," President Parker said. "But right now, you can see that I'm as surprised as anyone else in this room. I will make an enquiry and see what's going on," she said, reaching for her smartphone on the table.

But before she could pick it up, another tremor went through the room. This time it was much stronger and rattled everyone in their seats. President Parker almost slid off her chair but was quick enough to grab onto the side of the table, temporarily righting herself.

However, her folder and smartphone slipped off the table and fell to the floor. Bewildered, she bent over carefully to pick them up. As she did, she saw the other dignitaries in the room scrambling to pick up their belongings too.

When the other delegates had straightened up, they saw her staring at her phone.

"President Parker?" the Chinese President called out. "Is everything alright?"

President Parker looked up. "I don't know. I don't have any signal on my phone. Since when has this room been blocked from receiving signals?"

"Blocked?" the Russian President repeated. He took out his smartphone and looked at the screen. The expression on his face changed as he looked around. "She's right. I have no signal on mine either."

"President Parker, this is a serious breach of UN protocol. Why would you want to block our signals?" the French President asked.

"Block your signals?" President Parker repeated. "For goodness sake, didn't you hear what I just said?"

"Maybe there is another explanation to all of this," the UK Prime Minister said. "President Parker, can't you find out the cause of the tremors? Perhaps they could have affected our cellular networks."

"I would, if only–," President Parker began to say, but she suddenly stopped.

Every other delegate in the room noticed her staring out through the tall reinforced windows. They followed her gaze and, almost in unison, they gasped.

Through the window, they could see silver spacecrafts floating right outside the UN headquarters. There were seven of them, exactly the same in shape and design. They had formed a semi-circle directly facing the window on the floor of the building where the UN Security Council was meeting at that very moment.

From within the meeting room, President Parker and the other delegates were looking directly at the seven spacecrafts, hovering in mid-air. The spacecrafts seemed to be monitoring them intently.

"Those are the same beings we were talking about," the Russian President said.

"When did they get here?" the Chinese President asked.

President Parker shook her head. She glanced again at her smartphone. There was still no signal. She got up and walked briskly to the door. But when she tried the handle, the door wouldn't open. "What's going on here?" she asked, as she tried to open the door again.

"The door won't open?" the Russian President asked. "Wait. Let me give it a try." He tried to turn the handle but had no luck. Panicking, he barged into the door with his shoulder, but it still held firm. He tried again and again, but each of his efforts proved futile.

Bewildered, he turned to look at the other delegates. "Well, if President Parker wasn't here with us, I would have concluded that this was another ploy by the Americans to provoke us. But then, they wouldn't be so foolish as to try such trickery right here, inside the UN Headquarters."

"I'm glad you know that we aren't that foolish," President Parker said. "No one would want to do anything so stupid, not to mention something that is capable of destroying everything the world has been working on for all these years."

"And what is that?" a voice asked. "What have you all been working on for all these years?"

All the delegates turned towards the direction of the voice that had just spoken.

It wasn't one of the delegates who had said those words. Someone else was in the room with them. He was standing by the wall, and looked like just another ordinary person—aside from the skin-tight bodysuit that covered him from his neck down to his toes. It was simple and grey without any markings whatsoever.

President Parker gasped when she saw him. "Who are you? This is supposed to be a secure meeting room! How did you get in here?"

He turned and began to move towards President Parker. But as he moved, it was obvious that he wasn't walking. Rather, he was floating, effortlessly hovering about a foot above the floor.

As he floated towards her, the strange man continued to talk. "Tell me, President Parker, what is it that you claim to have been working on for all these years?"

President Parker glanced at the other delegates. They all looked shocked at the unfolding scenario.

"Look," President Parker continued, "I don't know who you are or what you want, but you should know that you are violating international peace protocols by being here right now."

"Violating?" the man asked. "What am I violating?"

"This is a peaceful gathering of the most powerful nations on this planet. Who are you and what are you doing here?" the Russian President demanded.

The man stopped in mid-air and turned to look at him. "You all seem confused as to the purpose of my being here. How interesting. Not too long ago, while my colleagues and I were on the fringes of your planet, we were deliberating the possible outcome of my intrusion on your meeting today. It's funny, isn't it? I mean, your reactions being just as we had anticipated."

"You knew we were going to be having this meeting today?" President Parker asked.

The Russian President glanced at his counterparts. "This is a serious breach of our protocols! How did you come across such highly classified information? No one in the entire world is supposed to know about this meeting."

The mysterious being smiled. "No one, except me and my entourage. And do you know why we know about this meeting? Do you know how we knew that Earth's most powerful leaders would be in this particular room at this particular time?" he asked, turning around in mid-air to look at the five delegates in the room. But no one offered a response. "It's because you are the same people who sent us here."

The Russian President stepped forward angrily. "What is the meaning of this? How could we have sent you when we don't even know who you are?"

"That's what you think, but it's true. Very true, indeed. You are the same people who passed the resolution to have my entourage and I come here, today, at this exact time, to meet with you," the being replied calmly.

"This is completely crazy," the Chinese President said. "Are we going to just stand here, listening to this person spout all this nonsense?"

The being pointed a finger at her. "What else are you going to do? Are you thinking of confronting me?"

President Parker waved at her fellow counterparts. "Ladies and gentlemen, I think this is not the time to raise issues with this person. There is virtually nothing we can do to get out of this situation. Why don't we see what we can learn from him?"

The Russian President nodded. "I have no choice but to agree with you, President Parker. I'm sure that this is not some kind of gimmick by your people to hold us all hostages. Let's learn what we can from him."

The other delegates in the room nodded as well.

The being smiled as he looked back at them. "That's an excellent decision. But, then again, why am I not surprised? After all, you are the world's most powerful leaders. And that means that, at any given moment, your action or inaction could determine the fate of your planet. Just as it has done right now."

"Could you please just tell us what is going on?" President Parker said. "Who are you and why are you here?"

"My name is Davius from Planet Xanadu and I am a member of Deep Probe, an elite research and study group based at NASA."

President Parker frowned. "Deep Probe? A study group at NASA? I've never heard of this group before."

"No, you haven't. And that's because right now, it doesn't exist. But very soon you will request and approve the founding of our unit," Davius smiled.

"Very soon?" President Parker repeated.

"Well, in exactly three years."

"Three years?" President Parker asked. She pointed at the seven floating spacecrafts that were outside the window. "Are you saying that you and all those came from the future?"

"Yes, Madam President. We are from thousands of years in your future."

The Russian President shook his head. "What future?"

Davius pointed at all the five delegates. "Yours, Mr. President. Your collective future several thousands of years from today."

"But that doesn't make any sense. How can you be from our collective future?" the Chinese President asked.

"Three years from today, you—the five of you who are sitting in this room before me—will agree to send some of your people to a new planet. You will send a group of scientists with thousands of embryos to inhabit a new planet, and you give them a mission. In a recorded message, you ask people from the future to return to this day to occupy Earth. This is the reason my team and I have been sent here—to carry out your instructions."

"That's impossible!" President Parker said. "How can we be the ones to issue such an instruction? How could we ever decide to allow anyone to colonize Earth?"

"But that's what happens; all five of you unanimously agree to pass that resolution," Davius said.

"And what would the aim of such a Council resolution be?" President Parker asked.

"It's simple. The present-day Earth needs to be taken over from you all today, in order to prevent you from destroying it tomorrow," Davius announced.

President Parker gasped. "Take over? You mean you *are* invading our planet?"

Davius shook his head. "No, I'm not invading your planet. Let's just say that we're taking over the administration of this planet from you, the world's most powerful leaders."

"A coup?" the Russian President exclaimed. "Why am I not surprised, President Parker? Just like my Chinese counterpart and I had suggested, these beings didn't come in peace. They had an agenda, which we now know was to take over Earth. We should have initiated an attack protocol rather than wasting all this time deliberating."

"Even if you had attacked us, what do you think you would have achieved?" Davius asked. "Complete failure. You cannot attack an enemy you know nothing about."

"How do you know so much about us?" exclaimed the French President.

"I know everything about you because I'm from your future," Davius replied.

"But how can you claim to be from our future? How can you say that we were the ones who sent you here when we don't even know anything about you?" the French President asked.

"The same question again," Davius sighed. "Alright, I'll give you a brief summary. You see, three years from now, the world will not be as you know it today. What is the objective of your Council?"

"Maintaining world peace," President Parker replied.

"Yes. It's a noble objective. But it doesn't last long. Not as long as you expect, anyway. In fact, about three years from now, the world will descend into a serious crisis and war will be imminent between several nations," Davius said.

The Russian President glanced at his Chinese counterpart. "Why doesn't this sound unfamiliar? And I'm guessing that China and Russia will stand together?"

Davius shook his head. "You will not take sides with China in this crisis. Previous alliances will be broken down completely. It will happen so quickly and so suddenly. And by the time you all realize it; there will be a full-blown crisis across the world."

"That doesn't sound too pleasant. What happens then?" the UK Prime Minister asked.

"That's when you all decide to send exploration and re-settlement teams to another planet," Davius replied.

"What's the reason for that? Aren't we supposed to have been fighting?" the Russian President asked.

"Yes, but you all still agree to take counter-measures that will ensure the preservation and continued survival of the human race. You know that the fate of the planet is at stake. World-wide war will surely wipe out the entire human race as you know it. This is why in the future, you decide to send the exploration and resettlement teams to find and populate another planet, so that in the event that Earth is destroyed, that planet would serve as a replacement to Earth today."

The Chinese President shook her head. "This story is ridiculous. You say we are all at war, and yet we somehow can still agree to take such precautionary measures? Why don't we simply agree not to fight in the first place?"

"That's an excellent question. But when greed and selfishness cloud the reasoning of leaders, what do you expect to happen?"

"A worldwide crisis," The UK Prime Minister replied. "And when is this supposed to happen?"

"About three years from now," Davius replied.

"And when it does, what else happens?" President Parker asked.

"Well, it turns out that your worst fears come true. Earth falls into full-scale war. The devastation and destruction is unimaginable. It's something that none of you could have expected, and none of you are prepared to experience, or even survive."

"And that's why you are here, right?" President Parker asked. "To warn us of what the future will hold if we don't take drastic measures to ensure lasting peace?"

Davius shook his head. "No."

President Parker looked surprised. "No?"

"No, President Parker. We aren't here to warn you about anything. As I said earlier, we are here to take over planet Earth."

"But what do you stand to gain by taking over our planet?" the Chinese President asked.

"We stand to gain everything; Earth will be safe, all of its people will be safe, and all your resources will be safe as well."

"Our resources?" the Russian President asked. "Aren't you from the future? What do you need our resources for?"

"What else do people need resources for? For survival, of course," Davius said.

President Parker shook her head. "I don't want to believe any of this. I refuse to believe any of this."

Davius turned to her. "Refuse? But how can you refuse? You are the same people that sent us back to take over Earth."

"I agree with President Parker," the Russian President said. "You could be anybody; you could've been sent to cause confusion among the world's ruling powers."

"Could I? Okay, maybe you all need to see this to be convinced."

Davius raised his left hand and began to turn a dial on what appeared to be a high-tech device on his wrist. After doing so, he pointed his left hand at the nearby wall. The delegates in the room were bewildered when a blue beam of light suddenly appeared from the device. The beam of light hit the wall he was pointing at.

The world leaders moved back in confusion and fear.

President Parker reached for her smartphone, but there was still no signal. Frustration and anger washed over her, but she had no choice but to put it aside and watch on.

The beam formed a blue circle of light where it hit the wall. Then, the color within the circle began to change gradually from blue to silver. As it turned to silver, the light shifted and changed texture, suddenly forming a solid circle with a thin border. It now appeared to be a sort of round mirror hanging on the wall. The surface within the border was completely grey.

At that point, Davius pressed a dial on his device again and the blue beam disappeared. However, the strange mirror was still on the wall.

Davius turned and looked at the frightened delegates in the room. "President Parker, and other heads of governments," he said, pointing at the silver mass on the wall. "Behold a video recording made by yourselves in the distant future."

Initially, there was nothing but the mirror on the wall.

Then, the images began to appear. There was a room. The room was not empty; it had a table with five chairs. On the chairs sat five individuals.

As the delegates looked more closely at the mirror, they began to recognize the occupants of the room.

And as they recognized them, they gasped in disbelief. President Parker recognized herself first, then the other four delegates.

Slowly, President Parker stood up, transfixed by their images in the recording on the mirror. "What is this?" She asked, not believing what she was seeing.

But Davius didn't say anything. Rather, it was President Parker's image that spoke. "Hello, distinguished delegates. By the time you receive this message, a representative from the future will be in your presence. As such, I know the state of confusion and shock you must all be in at this moment."

President Parker held her head.

The recording continued. "Madam President, I expect you will be holding your forehead, trying to contain the pounding headache that is already rushing through you. Instead of continuing to suffer from that awful migraine, I would advise that you see a doctor as soon as possible. I know what it might degenerate into because I have experienced it already."

"Is this some kind of joke?" the Russian President asked.

"And if the Russian President is there," the image of the Russian President interrupted, "I believe that he will already be wondering if this could be a prank organized by his American counterpart to deceive him into giving up on further stockpiling his nuclear arms. Come on, Mr. President, you are far smarter than that. For once, stop thinking that your life is all about winning some sort of battle for supremacy against the United States. You and every other person in this room need to pay very careful attention to this recording."

The Russian President glanced at the Chinese President with confusion written all over his face. The Chinese President shook her head. "I'm not going to agree to any of this. It must be a prank."

At that moment, the image of the Chinese President spoke. "Madam President, what have you been able to do about your husband's cancer?"

The Chinese President gasped and looked at the other delegates in the room. "How? How did she know about my husband's cancer? That's a secret. Not even my closest advisors are aware of this!"

The image of the Chinese President continued to speak. "We are telling you all these things to prove to you that we are the same people as you, in this room today. Please pay very close attention to this recording."

The room became silent as the image of President Parker stood up and addressed them. "Our messenger must have already briefed you by now. But I'm sure you are still harboring doubts. However, the fact is that in a couple of years from now, your world as you know it will be consumed by a global crisis that will lead to its complete destruction."

"And in the process, your world will be destroyed. It will start disintegrating and falling apart in three years from this," the image of the French President said.

The image of the Russian President raised a hand. "But the saving grace will be the Deep Probe initiative, which you are all fortunate to initiate and launch just as the crisis starts getting out of hand."

"Once that mission is judged to be a success, you all decide that people can be sent back to Earth on this particular date and time, to stop the war from happening in the first place, because that is the only way to protect Earth from being destroyed," the image of the Chinese President said.

"And this is why we have sent our people from the future to you right now," the image of President Parker said. "A representative has been sent to take over Earth today for one major reason. That reason, as you must understand by now, is to ensure that Earth is not destroyed by us. This is why we have made this recording. We want you to simply hand over the administration of Earth—right here, right now—to the messenger and his team."

"This is extremely important," the image of the UK Prime Minister said. "We have collectively agreed that this is the only way to prevent you from becoming foolish enough to let the global crisis happen in the first place."

"So that's what we're supposed to do now?" President Parker asked. "Simply hand Earth over to you, Davius?"

Davius nodded. "It's for the good of humanity, Madam President."

"You have to cooperate with the messenger and the Deep Probe initiative as they take over your present-day Earth," the image of President Parker continued. "And believe me, Madam President; it's for the good of humanity that you'll be doing so."

Suddenly, the Chinese President gasped. "My goodness, it's already started!" she shouted, pointing outside the window.

They were all in a state of confusion and bewilderment as they turned their attentions to the scene outside the window.

The skies were now filled with thousands of spacecrafts. They seemed to be falling from the clouds above, like raindrops towards the ground—flying through buildings, sidewalks and walkways.

Soon, the streets were sprawling with what seemed to be thousands of beings like Davius. They were moving around with practiced ease, entering buildings, escorting people out of the offices, and herding them into the streets. Loud announcements called out from the spacecrafts, calmly asking people not to panic.

"We come in peace. Do not panic. We are taking over Earth for the good of humanity."

People were running around hysterically at the apocalyptic sight in their midst.

The dignitaries in the room shook their heads. Some of them simply buried their heads in their hands, while the US President and the UK Prime Minister just stared out the window. It was as if they were searching for something, or perhaps hoping to find answers to the many questions that were plaguing their minds at that moment.

President Parker turned to her colleagues. They were speechless, frightened, and confused. She touched her forehead again and sighed. "Well, what can we do?" she asked as she sat down heavily. "Earth is being invaded by humans."

CHAPTER 3

The phone on the desk started to ring. The president picked it up. "President Parker speaking."

"Hello, Madam President."

"Mr. President, is that you?"

"Yes, madam. I'm calling from my office in the Kremlin."

"How is Russia today?"

"Well, what can I say? More spaceships are coming with more soldiers every day."

"We are facing the same thing, and I believe it's the same all over the world."

"How far have you gone with the directives that Davius gave us?"

"Are you referring to the orders that we should cancel all military activities?"

"Yes."

"What do you really want to know?"

"I just thought we could compare notes."

"Compare notes? Are you serious? You know, this isn't like before, when we were trying to outrace each other in a nuclear arms race."

The Russian President chuckled. "The good old days."

"Yes, the so-called good old days that led to the invasion of Earth by people from the future?"

"We really should've known that something like this might happen."

"We should've, but we didn't. And now Earth is how it is, run by these Future People. And what are we now? Rather than being the most powerful leaders in the world, we are now merely passive rulers who report to Davius on everything. Anyway, honestly speaking, there is nothing to tell you that isn't public information, easily accessible by any ordinary citizen out there on the road. Like other nations of the world, we in the US are already complying completely with all of the directives that Davius gave us."

"All of them?"

"Yes, of course. All of them."

"You mean you've also terminated all research centers for weapons development?"

"Mr. President, do you think we would even dare disobey? We are no longer researching or developing any weapons. All our nuclear missiles and armaments have been handed over."

"So it's true then? All the reports I see in the media about every nation in the world complying with the directive—even the almighty USA."

"Yes, Mr. President. Even the almighty USA. Have you already made the announcement to your people?"

"Yes, I have. It was a direct order from the Future People to all of us on Earth, so they have no choice other than to comply with it. I have already told them that no country has any weapons because all world leaders have been forced to discontinue all military activities and hand over all their weapons."

"And the termination of all research centers and activities in weapons design and development? Have you complied with that directive as well?"

"Absolutely, Madam President. We don't research or develop any weapons here in Russia anymore. And how are the American people taking everything so far?"

"Just as they've been instructed, they are all calm and complying with each order that is being given."

"They are complying easily?"

"Do they have a choice? Do any of us have a choice? Of course they're complying. I suppose that since the Future People came with a promise of lasting peace—peace that we never had before, because of our stupid nuclear games—our people have had no choice than to stay calm and see how things pan out. No one is living in the fear of a nuclear war anymore."

The Russian President sighed. "Yes, you're right Madam President. Even here in Russia, my people seem to be unusually calm and happy. The promise of peace is really something that everyone has always wanted, but never had."

"But it's not as if we have much choice now, Mr. President."

"You're right. In all our cities around the world, there are armed Future People."

"Yes, they are virtually everywhere—and when I say everywhere, I mean *everywhere*. Like I said before, Mr. President, we brought this situation upon ourselves and the entire world."

"I got a memo from Davius himself this morning."

"About the speech he plans on making at noon today? Yes, I got it too."

"What do you think he is going to say?"

President Parker laughed. "Come on, do you think I get that kind of information? How would I know?"

"What a pity, Madam President. The US has always been known for its sophisticated intelligence agency. I remember a time when there was nothing, absolutely nothing, not a single piece of information that you didn't have access to. In today's world, you are no more than a mere observer and a simple spectator."

"Yes, thank you, Mr. President, for reminding me of the so-called glorious past of the US. But that's just what it is now, the past and nothing else."

"I'm not trying to goad you; no, not at all. I'm just reflecting aloud, that's all."

"I see. But whether it is a reflection or a goad, you are talking about my country here, Mr. President."

"Your country? Or your former country? Aren't we simply figureheads in our respective domains? The Future People are the ones running the show now. We simply stay put to give an impression of normalcy. But every head of government in every country around the world, know the real truth about who is really in charge."

"Yes, and this fact should already be obvious to ordinary citizens out there on our streets too. They are all aware of the suspension of military activities. They have heard the announcements made on behalf of Davius, and they have seen the spaceships and the armed Future People in their midst. Does it take a nuclear scientist to deduce that things have seriously changed?"

"No, it doesn't Madam President. We've all been thrown back a hundred years into the past. A world that was so advanced is now on the brink of extinction. I can't believe this! It's as if we have become living witnesses to a horror movie. How do we get out of this mess?"

"Is there any getting out? We're all stuck in this living nightmare. And there's nothing we can do about it."

"You might be right. Well, let's see how things go. I have to go now, Madam President. It was nice talking to you."

"And to you, Mr. President." As soon as the line went dead, she sighed. It was a sigh of helplessness and defeat.

CHAPTER 4

The television screen turned on. It showed Davius himself, wearing his full grey bodysuit. He sat on an elegant brown leather armchair. Standing on each side was an armed man and an armed woman. It wasn't possible to tell where the video was being taken, because it was in a simple room without windows. Davius was looking directly into the camera.

President Parker sank deeper into her seat as she watched him.

Davius cleared his throat. "Fellow people of Earth. I have already made this speech before, but for the sake of clarity I'm going to repeat it. My colleagues and I are from the future. We don't mean any harm to anyone on Earth. Our reason for coming here is to prevent a future war, and to bring peace and prosperity to Earth. To achieve that, we have a list of rules that everyone must follow. By now, you must all have already been informed by your respective heads of government about the new situation here on Earth. I'm Davius from Planet Xanadu. My fellow colleagues and I have taken full charge of ushering Earth into a better future."

Davius paused at this point, as if allowing time for his words to sink into the consciousness of his listeners. "Wherever you are watching this broadcast—whether on your phone, computer or TV—I assure you that it is for the good of Earth that we are here. We have come to bring you all peace and prosperity, the two things that have been lacking from Earth ever since the first two world wars. In fact, it is accurate for me to say that since then, the world has drawn closer to war and insecurity than it has ever been before. And this is why we are here—to prevent the world from succumbing to an inevitable end."

Davius paused again before he continued. "For those of you who are used to the Internet, TV, and other forms of entertainment, I have some bad news for you. After this broadcast, you will no longer have access to these things again. That is one of the rules we have to implement to ensure that we can maintain everlasting peace and security on Earth. There will be no freedom of media or freedom of speech.

"Effective from this moment, there will be a twelve-hour curfew all over the planet. Everyone is expected to remain behind closed doors from sunset to sunrise. During the curfew period, no forms of gatherings will be tolerated. Everyone will be closely monitored, and any violators will be punished with life imprisonment. Please note that this situation is only transitional. We don't mean any harm to anyone. We are here for our collective good and the good of all humanity. You will be hearing more from me in the coming days. Thank you."

Just then, the President's phone started ringing.

"Hello?"

"Madam President, did you hear it? Did you hear what Davius said?"

"Yes, I did, Mr. President. Something tells me that you are not too happy about it in Russia."

"Happy? Who is talking about being happy here, Madam President? This is the state of the world we are talking about. Davius has effectively taken over our planet!"

"Has he? Tell me something that I don't already know."

"But this can't be! Can this really be happening?"

President Parker allowed her gaze to wander towards one of her windows. She saw a spacecraft hovering over her lawn. She could remember that not too long ago, she used to enjoy walking across the lawn of the White House, just to get a bit of fresh air. And on those days, there would be nothing but a clear blue sky above her. Now, if she ventured to walk outside on the same lawn, there would be no clear blue sky above her; all she would see would be the spaceships from the future.

"Madam President?"

"What do you want me to say, Mr. President?"

"My goodness gracious! If anyone in my government had ever told me that such an incident would happen in my own time, I would have locked them away and thrown away the key. And we were, thinking that Russia's greatest threat was the United States. Never in our wildest imagination would we have guessed that our greatest threat was actually, actually, actually—"

"Ourselves?"

"I cannot even get myself to say it, Madam President. I still can't believe that this is happening to us."

"We'd better get used to the idea."

"I understand. There is no point denying reality, especially the one that is unfolding right before our very eyes. My major concern right now is how my people are going to react to everything that's happening right now."

"You'd better make sure that they don't try any form of opposition," warned President Parker. "We all heard what Davius said. Even though they have come in peace, they will not tolerate any breakdown of law and order."

"And does anyone have any idea of what the situation might be in other parts of the world? Africa, Asia, South America?"

"With all media shut down, we can only guess," President Parker sighed.

"And with our entire governments out of operation, this is a nightmare."

"Yes, it is. I had to disband my entire cabinet. So it's basically just me now, taking orders from the Future People."

"No, not just you, Madam President, we are all in the same boat—all the world leaders. We all had to disband our respective governments, remember?"

"Yes, you're right, we all did. Now, we report directly to Davius. This is really a nightmare that we're living in."

CHAPTER 5

At that very moment, the mothership was hovering above the skyline of New York. Davius was sitting in his office on board the ship. On the wall were several screens. As he was watching them, the indicator on his door beeped three times and there was a soft buzz. The door slid into the panel and a woman walked into his office. She was wearing the same grey bodysuit as Davius and had a holster attached to the belt on her hips. She was holding a device in her hands. Davius looked away from the screens as she approached.

"Commander Davius," the woman said. "Have you seen these updates from China?"

"What updates?"

"These," she said pointing the device towards the wall.

Immediately, a new screen on the wall turned on. On it, Davius could see an urban area with several high-rise buildings and some car parks. There were several queues of people, mostly adults. They were all walking with their hands behind their backs. They were all handcuffed. By their sides were the Future People, in their unmistakable grey bodysuits, armed with automatic laser rifles.

"Is this live?".

"Yes, Commander. It started about ten minutes after your last worldwide broadcast."

"In Beijing?"

"Yes, Commander. They just started to gather on the streets. When we confronted them, they stated that they wanted to exercise their fundamental human right of peaceful protest against the takeover of earth."

"Fundamental human rights indeed. Well, I'm pleased that our forces responded very quickly to this attempted breach of public peace."

"Thank you, Commander. For now, they remain detained on the streets in handcuffs. Our troops are awaiting further instructions on what should be done."

Davius rubbed his chin. "What else is there to do? First of all, we make an example of them."

"An example of them, Commander?"

"Yes, by publicizing what has just happened in Beijing. Let the whole world see what the Chinese people were about to do."

"Of course, Commander. That means we would need to temporarily restore the media systems in order to stream everything across the whole world."

"Yes, yes, do that. Then while the world is watching, we'll begin to ship them off to Planet Xanadu. Make sure the entire process is covered on live television and social media. I want everyone to see that I'm very serious about our zero-tolerance for any kind of opposition to our policies."

The woman nodded. "Yes, Commander, I understand. Let me contact our troops in Beijing right away."

"And tell our media group to set me up for another worldwide broadcast," Davius directed. "I want to make the broadcast as soon as our troops have begun to ship those dissidents to Planet Xanadu."

"Yes, Commander, I will do so immediately."

After she had left, Davius turned his attention back to the latest screen. His troops were still present when drones began to appear in the streets, though the troops were not alarmed. But Davius could see that the other people were becoming restless at the sight of the small flying objects zooming overhead.

The intercom on his desk buzzed and Davius pressed the beeping blue button. "Yes?"

"Commander, our troops in Beijing are already rounding up the prisoners. A carrier ship has just been deployed to evacuate them. Until its arrival, a team of broadcast drones will monitor the area."

"Good. They may commence the broadcast of the incident all over the world."

"Yes, Commander. We were wondering when you would like to make your own broadcast."

"It can be done now. I want my broadcast to be a live feed, interspersed with images of the prisoners."

Davius relaxed into his seat and continued to watch the unfolding scene in Beijing.

CHAPTER 6

Back at the White House, President Parker was surprised to see her television screen turn on.

She looked up and saw the queues of people lined up. She also saw the armed troops and the hovering drones.

Suddenly, that was replaced with another image. It was Davius sitting in his office. He was smiling into the camera. "Good day again, my fellow people of Earth. I believe you may be surprised that I have not only restored your access to all media channels, but that I am also making another broadcast not even an hour after the first one."

The image changed to that of Beijing, as the people in the queues were being surrounded by the armed troops.

"Well, there is a good reason for all this," Davius continued. "What you are witnessing right now is a live feed from Beijing, China. We understand that few minutes ago, some Chinese citizens thought it's wise to go against my earlier instructions about the complete curfew from sunrise to sunset. They not only disregarded this order, but went ahead with protests and civil disturbances."

Davius paused as the cameras zoomed in on the background. A huge cargo ship could be seen landing in the foreground, not far from where the troops were standing with the prisoners. It looked like a pair of warships connected to each other by round cylinders. The ship had several masts sticking out of its hulls and on its bridge, where some of the troops could be seen standing. Like their counterparts on the ground, they were armed with automatic laser rifles.

"What you are seeing on your various screens at the moment," Davius continued in a voice over, "is the arrival of one of our many cargo ships. It's going to ferry these dissidents, these troublesome folks to Planet Xanadu. Once they are there, they will serve life sentences during which they will be re-educated, not just about how to live peacefully amongst other people, but also about how to follow instructions given by lawful authorities."

Gangways had dropped from the sides of the ship. Troops were stationed by each side of the gangways, both on the ground and on the ship itself. One by one, each of the handcuffed protesters could be seen filing onto the gangways that led on to the cargo ship.

"This is what will happen to anyone who tries to organize or join any form of protest, march or civil disobedience," Davius reappeared on the screen. "They will be shipped off to Planet Xanadu to serve life sentences with hard labor. Now, I know you may be thinking that we are being harsh in our approach to guaranteeing peace. But mark my words—everything we are doing is for your own good. So I implore everyone to take a positive view of what's happening in Beijing. Let it be a lesson to anyone who might be harboring ideas of protest or rebellion. Thank you."

The image of Davius disappeared from the screen, but the live feed continued, showing the prisoners being marched onto the cargo ship. In no time, they had all boarded the ship. The gangways were then drawn in one after the other.

A few troops still remained on the ground, watching as the spaceship lifted from the ground and headed off into space.

President Parker's phone started ringing. She reached for it. "Yes?"

"Did you see that? Did you?"

"Yes, I did. Of course I did, Mr. President."

"You did?"

"Of course I did. Everything is being broadcasted live, and worldwide," she chuckled.

"Why are you laughing at me?"

"I can't help but find all this a bit funny, Mr. President."

"Funny? What's so funny about our fellow people being rounded up and shipped to another planet?"

"No, that's not what I find funny, Mr. President. It's you."

"Me? How am I being funny?"

"Come on, you know what I'm talking about. Not so long ago, the USA and Russia weren't on the best of terms. We weren't exactly buddies. And yet, here you are calling me almost every minute, wanting to talk about what's going on in the world? Come on, even with all that has happened, I'm sure the entire world would be very surprised to learn of this sudden renewed relationship between the former superpowers of our planet."

"Please, please, please, Madam President! I don't have time for such jokes. This is serious, honestly. They're taking our people away!"

"Technically, it's the Chinese people."

"Madam President, they are human beings and they are being carted away to who knows where?"

"Planet Xanadu, that's where they are being taken to. And from the name, it sounds like a really nice place."

"How can you tell? Have you been there before?"

"Calm down, Mr. President. So far, all we know is that Davius says he is a peace-loving person. I blame those protesters for daring to stand up to them in the first place. They should have listened and followed the new rules. That way, none of this would have happened in the first place."

"So, they deserve what has happened to them?"

"That's not what I said, Mr. President. And by the way, since when did you care about what was happening to other people in the world outside of Russia? I have never known you to be so affectionate and caring towards other nations."

"You wouldn't understand, Madam President. Times change and people change with them."

"I see. Especially desperate and unpredictable times like these?"

"Yes, you may be right about that."

"Come on, Mr. President. Maybe all these measures will have a better impact on society as a whole."

"What do you mean?"

"I mean, with all these restrictions in place, I'm very sure that crime levels are going to reduce drastically all over the world."

"Crime levels?"

"Yes, crime levels. When curfews are in place, who would have the audacity to go out and commit a crime?"

"Perhaps. But if anyone does commit a crime, what will happen to them?"

"You mean whether there's something worse than being shipped off to Planet Xanadu for life? Well, I really can't say. But then, wouldn't it be really foolish of anyone to consider any criminal activity when all of Earth has been taken over by the Future People?"

The Russian President sighed. "I just don't know what to think anymore. But for our sakes and the sake of all humanity, I hope no one does anything foolish."

CHAPTER 7

In the following months, things started to calm down. The people of Earth started to get used to the situation on their planet. There seemed to be law and order everywhere. Even Davius and his colleagues were at ease.

However, unbeknownst to Davius and his colleagues, the citizens of the United Kingdom were becoming restless. Even though the crime levels had decreased, some people were still unhappy. Unlike those who were content to live under strict conditions in exchange for peace, there were those who felt like prisoners. They didn't like the fact that they were always being watched, or that the media and the Internet were exclusively controlled by the Future People. Under the pretext of moving from place to place, these groups of people began to meet in the subways and underground trains.

They would board the trains and occupy selected coaches to share their ideas, perfecting ways in which they could cause civil disturbances around the United Kingdom. They already knew what happens to dissenters. Anyone who didn't comply with the directives of the Future People would serve life imprisonment on Planet Xanadu. But even that thought didn't bother them as they continued to meet and plan.

One early morning at 2am, the alarm on the mothership woke Davius from his sleep. He jumped up and quickly got dressed before hurrying over to the control room.

"I heard the alarm. What's going on? What's happening?" he demanded.

One of the many officers in the control room turned to him. "We've just been informed of a riot that's taking place in London."

"A riot in London?"

"Yes, Commander. Five hundred of our soldiers have either been injured or killed," the officer said. "And the numbers are rising even as we speak."

This is unbelievable! Davius thought. *How could they do such a thing when we are in control? They broke the curfew. They must have planned it some time ago.*

Davius rubbed his chin as he gazed at the screens. "From what I can see on these live feeds, they must've been very organized to succeed on such a large scale."

The screens displayed images of central London, with the unmistakable Big Ben and the London Eye in the background. Several people were being lined up in the streets, with sleek spaceships not too far above them. Armed Future People in grey bodysuits could be seen moving amongst the people, carrying laser rifles that made them look very formidable and intimidating. The dissidents were walking in single file with their hands raised up high above their heads, though some had their hands cuffed behind them. There was no discrimination. Men and women, young and old were marched along at gunpoint. Drones were also flying amongst the people, hovering a couple of feet above their heads, relaying the incident as a live feed to the various media channels for the whole world to see.

Davius quickly left the control room to start a live broadcast in his office.

"Hello, fellow people of Earth," he greeted. "The feed you can all see now is live from London. Despite how we dealt with the protests in Beijing several months ago, certain people in London still thought that they knew better. They not only took matters into their own hands, but even took it a step further by engaging in civil disobedience and rioting."

The images of London showed that the streets were now occupied by several of Davius' troops, all fully-armed and formidable as they led people away in handcuffs.

"These people are going to be severely dealt with," Davius continued, "Because they violently protested during a time of peace, when everyone else was following our directives.

"We are not going to take such insolence lightly. No, not at all. These protesters are going to be imprisoned with life sentences with hard labor. Yes, this will serve as a severe deterrent to all of those who think they can test our resolve and patience.

"Once again, I'm going to give this warning to every single person here on Earth. If anyone dares disobey my earlier directives forbidding gatherings, protests, riots, and civil disobedience, they should know that they will spend the rest of their lives carrying out hard labor on Planet Xanadu.

"Any citizen from any nation that wants to engage in such unbecoming acts will only have themselves to blame for the consequences. Let this be a lesson to everyone everywhere. Thank you."

***

Davius got to a door that was manned by a man and a woman, both were dressed in similar bodysuits to Davius. They held automatic laser rifles and had packs of ammunition attached to their belts. As they saw Davius approach, they saluted him. Davius nodded at them. He waited while the door behind the armed guards slid open and disappeared into the wall. He then walked into a large room and the door slid shut behind him.

In front of him was a huge widescreen. On it, he could see a long rectangular table. Behind the table were three women and two men. They were not dressed in the same bodysuits as Davius and his troops. Rather, they were all wearing white gowns that draped down to their ankles. The sleeves, hems, and necklines of the gowns had beautiful embroidery in green and yellow. The patterns of the embroidery were elaborate and impressive. Gold crowns with large blue jewels rested on their heads, and on each of their fingers they wore gold rings. They were the rulers of Davius' home planet, Planet Xanadu.

Davius walked up to the widescreen and bowed his head slightly. "Distinguished Council of Elders, I greet you all. I was made to understand that you required my presence?"

"Yes, we do, Commander Davius," one of the women said. "And we apologize for calling you with such short notice."

"I understand," Davius said. "I am sure that whatever it is that the Council needs me for must be quite urgent for you to request for my presence so urgently."

"Yes, it is, Commander Davius," the same woman said. She pointed at the wall behind Davius with one of her ringed fingers. As she did this, the wall turned into another huge widescreen television.

"While we were in Council, we received the live feed of the revolution in the United Kingdom," one of the men said. "We were very concerned that such an incident could have been planned at all, let alone implemented."

"Can you tell this Council for a fact that you are in absolute control of the affairs of this planet?" one of the women asked.

Davius nodded calmly. "I am sorry that you all had to witness these temporary setbacks. I have to agree that the dissent in Beijing and London was quite unexpected. We never expected that the humans of this era would behave in that way despite my explicit warnings. But as you may have already seen, we quickly took charge in both instances. Nothing of the sort will happen again."

"We saw the footage of the actions you took, Commander, and we are satisfied," the second man stated, "actually we would like to congratulate you on your progress so far, and in view of this, we want you to move on to Plan B, effective immediately."

CHAPTER 8

President Parker stood by one of the windows in her office, overlooking the freshly cut lawns of the White House. In her hand was a cup from which she was sipping lemon tea. She could see a spacecraft hovering over the lawn, like a huge bee eyeing the petals of a flower it was about to dive into. Except that this was no bee. This was a spaceship from the future—their future, the future of all humanity.

She was already used to seeing this particular spaceship positioned right over her favorite view of her lawn. There were others positioned at various spots around the expansive grounds of the White House, but this one in particular was of interest to her that afternoon.

It always remained in that one same spot, floating in mid-air—formidable, imposing, and unmoving. It reminded her of a giant statue or symbol.

Symbol of what? The present state of affairs on planet Earth? Or of humanity?

"Would you like more tea, Madam President?"

She blinked and turned to see the two orderlies that Davius had assigned to her. But she knew it wasn't just her. Every head of government across the world had similar orderlies assigned to them, so her case wasn't peculiar. Neither was it much different for any other ordinary citizen of the world. Wherever people went, they were sure to come across the heavily armed troops, walking amongst them—at schools, in restaurants, at parks—virtually everywhere that people were used to going to. It became almost impossible to go anywhere without seeing the Future People troops. Their grey bodysuits had become ubiquitous, like the yellow taxi cabs that plied New York's streets, or traffic lights at most intersections.

President Parker nodded. "Yes please."

As the first orderly poured tea into her cup, the President caught sight of the orderly's belt. It wasn't a normal belt; it was quite different and somewhat special. Attached to it were some canisters and a purse. But those were not what had caught her attention. It was the butt of the automatic pistol. It stuck out visibly from where it was holstered at the top of the belt, with its smooth barrel poking down.

"So, must you always be armed around me?"

The woman blinked. She turned to her colleague, who gazed back at her with that same empty expression that the President had known them to wear as if it was their makeup. They always seemed to have a distant yet calm looks in their eyes at all times.

"Yes, Madam President," the first orderly replied. "We are your security detail and we must be armed at all times."

"I know you must be armed at all times, but this is the White House. And besides, your troops are everywhere here—in the corridors, in the hall, even on my lawn outside. Why still carry these things around me?"

"It is for your safety, Madam President."

President Parker nodded and took a sip of her tea. "Yes, so you keep on saying, like a broken record. And funnily enough, that's exactly what your Commander keeps telling me and the other heads of government around the world. Everything that's being done is for our safety."

"Would you like more tea, Madam?"

President Parker glanced into her cup. "No, not yet. I still have some in my cup. And by the way, aren't you supposed to just watch over my security? Since when did you become my new personal butler?"

"We are here to ensure—"

"Yes I know," President Parker waved aside her remark. "My safety."

She turned her attention outside the window, not bothering to gauge the reaction of the orderlies. She sighed. They were simply all over her, always with her everywhere she went.

They aren't just ensuring my safety, she mused. *They're part of Davius' surveillance systems, informing him of whatever the heads of government are doing.*

Surveillance systems, indeed!

As she continued to watch the unmoving spacecraft, she recalled the day that Davius and his troops arrived on Earth. After she and her fellow delegates had been apprehended at the United Nations headquarters, they had all been sent back to their respective countries, accompanied by two security details each. And since then, things hadn't been the same. She knew from Davius' speeches that the mothership was based in New York, floating through the sky like some ominous reminder of the inevitability of its presence. She recalled seeing it on a couple of occasions when it had flown overhead. It was so large that it could cast a complete dark shadow over the White House whenever it passed, like some massive, dark rain cloud. Even if it was a clear sunny day, the mothership was capable of throwing any area into complete darkness since it could easily block out any sunlight.

But that was just the mothership. The other spaceships, like the one hovering over the lawns of the White House, were quite large and formidable as well. Those smaller ones had been charged with hovering much closer to the cities and streets, while the mothership stayed much higher up in the atmosphere.

After a while, she finished drinking her tea. As she moved to place her cup on the table, one of the orderlies stepped forward. "Is there anything else you need, Madam President?"

President Parker shook her head. "No, thank you. I'd like to retire for the day and get some rest now. That is, if it's alright with the two of you."

The two orderlies nodded as she walked to her bedroom and shut the door. She slid into her bed and closed her eyes.

She wasn't sure how long she must have slept. All she could tell was that while she was sleeping, she had felt a hand shaking her. At first she thought it was a dream. But when the shaking became more pronounced and insistent, she opened her eyes slowly, wondering what was going on.

She was shocked to see a man standing by her side. As she sat up in confusion and fear, the man held his hand over his lips, instructing her to be silent. He was dressed in a black, long-sleeved turtleneck and black trousers. His hands were concealed by black gloves and he was wearing a black ski mask. Even his boots were black. She couldn't help but wonder who he was and how he had gotten into her bedroom in the White House.

She nodded. She didn't know what to think as she watched the man walk to the window and peer outside. It was obvious that he was searching for something. But she wondered if he would see what he was searching for, considering that it was already night and everywhere outside was very dark. Seemingly satisfied, he left the window and walked softly to the door. He placed his head on the door to listen for a while before he turned the key and locked it.

He then walked back to the bed and sat down on its edge. He looked at her. "Madam President, I apologize for intruding on you and your privacy like this." His voice was hushed, as he made an effort to talk to her without detection.

President Parker felt herself relax a bit. She hadn't seen any weapons on the man and with the respectful way he was addressing her, she suspected that he wasn't there to harm or kill her. "Who are you and what are you doing here?" she asked in an equally low voice.

In response, the man pulled off his ski mask. President Parker gasped softly and covered her mouth with her hands, as if trying to stop herself from screaming out. "You?"

"Yes, Madam President. It's me, Jeffrey, your former Secretary of Defense."

"What are you doing here?"

"I had to see you at all costs, Madam President."

She shot a glance at the door. "How did you get into my room?"

Jeffrey grinned. "I can't tell you that, Madam President. But rest assured that no one else knows."

"No one else knows?"

"No, Madam President. No one else knows that I'm here and no one knows the route by which I was able to gain access to your room."

"I see. So what's my Defense Secretary doing in my bedroom?"

"Your former Defense Secretary, Madam President."

President Parker sighed as she rubbed her forehead. "Yes, you're right. But you know that I had no choice in doing what I did. It was a strict directive from Davius to all world leaders."

"Yes, I know, and so do my other colleagues. We heard the news and knew that there was nothing you could do."

"Well, just know that no matter what might have happened, you still remain my Defense Secretary to me."

Jeffrey shook his head. "I don't think you are in touch with reality, Madam President. Your Defense Secretary? When was the last time you held a cabinet meeting? When was the last time I gave you a memo about the latest threats affecting the United States? In fact, when was the last time you even saw me in person?"

President Parker gazed out of the window. She then turned her attention to the spaceship hovering in mid-air over the lawn. Jeffrey followed her gaze. "That spaceship outside over the lawn, is it always there?"

"Yes. Always. Every moment of the day."

"What an insult. We're talking about the White House, for crying out loud! From a symbol of stability and global power, they turned it into a mere shadow of its former self."

President Parker looked back at Jeffrey. "I'm sure you didn't come here to discuss how the Future People have changed the reputation of the White House, Defense Secretary."

He shook his head. "No, of course I didn't, Madam President. But before I even go any further, could you please stop calling me that?"

"Calling you what?"

"Defense Secretary."

"But that–"

"No, please just stop. That's not who I am anymore. Didn't you just say so yourself a while ago? We all know that the title doesn't even exist anymore. After the invasion, everything was scrapped. Apart from you dissolving the entire cabinet, they gave out the orders for the dismantling of formal government structures, before they clamped down heavily on all forms of military.

"All over the world, there is no longer any military infrastructure, weaponry, training, research or development of any kind. So why call me by a defunct title? It's not like you, Madam President. You and the other heads of government might still retain your titles, but the rest of us are now merely ordinary citizens."

President Parker rubbed her forehead. "Fine, I get your point. So what do I call you now?"

"Just my name. Is that okay?"

"Of course, Jeffrey. I haven't called you that since I personally nominated you to the Senate for confirmation when I took office."

Jeffrey smiled. "Yes. I'm glad you remember."

"Why did you come here today?"

Jeffrey moved closer, "the absurd realities of our present day existence."

"Well, we're living in a different time, that's for sure. Yes, things have changed."

"Not just changed, drastically changed. And it's terrible."

"Easy there, Jeffrey. You don't want to go voicing your opposition to Davius and his administration. He would–"

"He would what, Madam President?" Jeffrey cut in. "What is he really going to do about it? It's just my honest opinion about the situation of things—an opinion that I'm sure several other people share elsewhere in the world right at this very minute. Things are no longer as they used to be."

"They can't be the same, Jeffrey. We're living in the future."

"Yes, this is the future. But it's not a future that our humanity wanted. It's *their* future, the future that *they* want for us."

"And it's for our own good."

"Our own good, or their own good?"

President Parker shifted in the bed. "Everything they're doing is for our own good, Jeffrey. Surely you can see that."

"No, that's not true. And I can see *that*. I wouldn't blame you for having such a narrow vision of reality. After all, you and the other heads of government are supposed to be working for Davius and his people. But no matter where your present loyalties lie, it doesn't erase the fact that things are completely different now."

"And neither does it take away the fact that with Davius and his people around, things are getting better."

"Better? Did you just say 'better'?"

"Of course better! Take a look at crime rates. They have plunged lower than levels ever recorded anywhere."

"That's because everyone is too afraid to do anything."

"Then fear is good, if that's what it takes to eradicate crime."

"But how long will people be ruled by fear? How long can their freedom be replaced by laws that trap them in that cycle of perpetual fear? How long?"

"For as long as it's necessary."

"And how long is that?"

"You heard me the first time, Jeffrey. For as long as it's necessary."

"I don't believe this! You used to represent liberty, the dream humanity tries to achieve."

"That's in the past, Jeffrey. That's all in the past. This is the present, and this present has a new set of realities."

"Realities? What realities?"

President Parker waved her hand around. "The ones you can see with your very own eyes, Jeffrey."

"So you support what happened to the English and the Chinese? You support how your fellow human beings were shipped off to that planet?"

"Planet Xanadu."

"Whatever. It could be called Planet Elysium, Planet Eden, or Planet Heaven for all I care. What bothers me is that you support such a thing happening to other people in the first place."

"What is this, Jeffrey? Are you suggesting that I had anything to do with what happened to them?"

"Not just you, but you and your fellow world leaders."

"So that's what this visit is all about, to vent your anger at me and the other world leaders for supporting Davius? Well, I'm sorry to say that's where you are wrong, Jeffrey. Come on, don't tell me you're too enraged and blinded to realize that we are all mere puppets? We've become figureheads that report to Davius on a regular basis. We don't have any power to do anything anymore."

"But you all could voice your opinions to Davius, make him see things differently."

"And then what would happen? Tell me, Jeffrey, what do you think would happen? You want us all to get shipped off to Planet Xanadu?"

"But you wouldn't be sent there. And neither would anyone who raises their voice in opposition. We aren't rioting, nor are we engaging in a revolution, for that matter. We are only saying that we don't like what's happening."

"Well then good luck with that, Jeffrey. If you think you can make things change from the way they are to the way they should be, then you are definitely looking for trouble." She paused to glance out of the window. "You do know that one wrong move on your part and off you go."

"I'm not a fool, Madam President. If I was, I doubt you'd have nominated me as a Defense Secretary in the first place."

"Yes, I used to know that you weren't a fool. But with the way times have changed, I'm beginning to wonder if you have decided to become one."

Jeffrey chuckled heartily. "Come on, madam. You don't think I would ever do *that*."

"How would I know? I haven't seen you in a while now. Maybe you've been busy toying with the idea before you decided to come and visit me for validation. Well, I'm sorry but I can't validate such a crazy idea, especially not one involving one of my former trusted aides."

"Please just take it easy. I'm not thinking of *that*."

"I do hope not."

Jeffrey ran his hand through his hair. "It's just that I can't help but wonder sometimes. And when I do, I remember those times when we used to discuss military strategies in the Pentagon."

"Really?"

"Yes, when we used to analyze enemy threats, visualizing their possible modes of attacks and resource levels, that sort of thing."

"I see."

Jeffrey paused to look directly at her. "Do you, Madam President?"

"Yes, I do."

Jeffrey shook his head. "No, you don't, because if you did, you wouldn't be so calm about everything that's going on right now."

President Parker sighed. "Here we go again."

"No, seriously, I mean it. The similarities are so strong, when you look deeper into things."

"What are you talking about, Jeffrey?"

"From the analysis I've done, I'm very suspicious of what eventually became of those protesters from Beijing and London."

President Parker frowned. "What do you mean? They're all on Planet Xanadu."

"How can you be so sure?"

"Because that's what Davius said."

"And you're saying we should believe everything he tells us?"

"I don't understand Jeffrey. Why should we begin to doubt what he says?"

"Look, Madam President, have you thought about the possibility that everything he has been saying might not really be the true state of things?"

"What? Are you insane? Do you know what you're implying?"

"Yes, of course I know what I'm implying. What I'm saying is, what if everything that we've been told is all a big scam, a lie? What if nothing is as it appears?"

President Parker was shaking her head. "You really are insane, Jeffrey. Do you know that?"

"No, I'm not. I'm curious, and because of my years of experience and training as a military strategist, I'm forced to see things differently. And what I see is really disturbing. And anyone who can see what I see should also be disturbed, and perhaps as angry as I've been all this time."

"You don't know what you're saying, Jeffrey. You are simply deeply upset and disturbed. And that's a surprise, especially for someone who once was in charge of deciding the fates of entire armies and nations."

"Yes, I agree. But back in those days, I had to make those decisions for the overall good of the American people, our allies, and our interests. Now, as I look at what's happening, I'm gravely concerned because the actions and implications of Davius' activities are in direct opposition to all that they claim to represent."

"So, you think that Davius is not being honest with us?"

"He isn't, and I'm absolutely sure about that. Just take a look at what he said he did to those people. Why send the English rebels who violently protested to the same place as the Chinese dissidents who were marching peacefully? Does it make sense? Would you keep a pick-pocket in the same cell block as an armed robber?"

"But they were all sent to Planet Xanadu. That doesn't mean they were sent to the same holding facilities."

"They weren't. And do you know why? It's because they must have been killed."

"Jeffrey!"

"No, don't trivialize this. I'm serious. Those were people like you and me. And what did they do? They only stood up for their rights and yet they were killed. Killed, Madam President, not imprisoned as Davius is leading us to believe."

"Jeffrey, I don't want to hear this."

"But you have to. It's the truth."

"You don't know what you're saying. Were you there? Did any of Davius' troops tell you this?"

"Of course, none of them would tell me that. And I don't need them to either. The evidence is there for all to see—that's, for all those who aren't too frightened to see. I'm telling you, those people were all killed."

"Jeffrey, you don't know what you're saying."

"Look, it's not logical for the Future People to imprison all those who spoke up against their directives. Do you think they will continue to imprison any opposition group that springs up anywhere else in the world?"

"No one will oppose them openly again, not after what happened to the protesters in London and Beijing."

"If that's what you think, then it shows how disconnected you are with reality. You can't cage people the way that Davius and his troops have—instituting curfews, restricting movement, dismantling all media and social interaction, reducing life to the barest minimum—but still expect the public to be compliant and docile. Remember, these are people that have been used to associating with one another, and enjoying basic human freedoms. No, you can't expect them not to revolt."

"If they dare to consider such an option, then they would suffer the same fate."

"And be killed as well?"

"Jeffrey, what is it with this idea of yours? No one is being killed, they're being imprisoned."

"And you think that other people who engage in riots and such will continue to be shipped off the planet? Do you think it's feasible that the Future People would have sufficient facilities to imprison that many people? Do you?"

President Parker nodded. "Of course they can. Why not? They're from the future, aren't they? Are you going to use your knowledge of prison systems in our times to judge how theirs might be in the future? Aren't you making a mistake by even thinking in that way?"

"I'm not going to make such a comparison or evaluation because doing so would not be logical. However, what I can do, and what I've done so far, is to study what they've been doing and saying, and looking at the strategies that they claim to be working on. And all I can see is that everything is one big lie. It just doesn't add up at all. Trust me, those people have all been killed."

"I can't trust your judgment on that. And do you know why?"

"Because I no longer work for you as your Defense Secretary?"

"No, not because of that. It's because I seriously believe that you might be insane, and that you just don't know what you're saying."

Jeffrey shrugged. "You can think whatever you want about me. But I still insist that it's the truth. The Future People are slowly and systematically slaughtering our people, one by one."

"There's no logic in what you're saying, Jeffrey—do you know why? It's because they are here for our own good. They are here to maintain peace and order, to prevent us from falling into another World War. Do you know how many times I have chatted—did you hear that? *chatted*—with the Russian President in the past twenty-four hours? And I mean chatting like two good old friends, Jeffrey. The Russian President, for goodness sake! We're like good buddies now."

"That's part of the illusion that Davius has created in your mind."

"No, that's the reality of the situation he has brought to us. No more nuclear arms, no more military research and development. Just peace and order."

Jeffrey glanced at the spaceship that was hovering outside on the lawn. "Are they the reason?"

President Parker followed his gaze. "Are they the reason for what?"

"Are they the reason why you don't want to tell the truth, to admit the truth about what I'm saying?"

"Look, Jeffrey, they don't have anything to do with this. Even when I discuss matters with my fellow heads of government, we are very open about what we say, the ideas we share, and everything else. The presence of the spaceship outside doesn't hinder my discussions."

"Then why don't you want to see reason and admit that what I'm saying is true?"

"Because it isn't, Jeffrey. It simply isn't the truth."

Jeffrey got up to his feet. "Well, there's no need for me to keep hanging around here then."

"Where are you going?"

"I'm leaving."

"Just like that? You don't want to stay and have some tea with me, maybe we could even talk some more?"

"Talk about what?"

"Anything. Surely there must be other things we can talk about."

"Like what, Madam President? What else is there to talk about?"

"So you have to go?"

"Yes, maybe I will come around some other time."

"Some other time?"

"Yes, maybe by then you will have started seeing things the way I'm seeing them. Have a nice day."

"Jeffrey!"

"Yes, Madam President?"

"Look, you need to understand something very clearly."

"What's that, Madam President?"

"The Future People—Davius and the troops—they aren't our enemies. They're us. We were the ones who sent them here to our present time. They were sent here by us in the future to help us prevent our self-annihilation and destruction in another World War. They mean us no harm."

"So you support them."

"Maybe if I showed you something your opinion would change."

"What do you want to show me?"

President Parker picked up the remote control on a table nearby. She pointed it at the television.

"You still have access to television?" Jeffrey asked, as the television came on.

"No, this isn't live television. It's a video recording."

"A video recording of what?"

"Just watch and decide for yourself."

Jeffrey didn't sit down. He remained standing as the video began to play. It was the same video that President Parker and her colleagues had watched while they were in the United Nations Headquarters, just before they had all been sent back to their respective countries.

At the end of the video, Jeffrey snorted and shook his head vigorously. "That's nonsense. It's not real. It's a fake."

"Fake?"

"Yes fake. This is just another ploy by Davius to brainwash the people into believing his story. I'm sorry, but I'm not buying it."

"But it's real, Jeffrey. And it *is* the truth."

"No, Madam President. What's real to me is what I can see happening in the world around me today. And for your own good, I would suggest you and the other world leaders take control of the situation before it's too late."

President Parker scoffed. "And how do you propose we do that?"

"Take control of your country. Stand up and fight for all we have always stood for. Fight for our liberties, fight for our freedom, and fight these fraudsters who say they're from the future. Fight now before it's too late."

"Fight? What are we really going to be fighting for? These people are here for our greater good; the greater good of the entire human race. And the results of their intentions are already manifesting themselves. Life in general for people is far better now, crime rates have drastically reduced, all nations co-exist in harmony and peace; there are no conflicts, no wars, and no disputes anywhere."

Jeffrey pointed a finger at the President. "I am disappointed in you, Madam President. How could you be so fooled by these people? How could you?"

"I'm not fooled. It's you who is caught up with your false beliefs. Are you blind, Mr. Watson? You of all people should know all the risks we faced before the arrival of the Future People."

"You don't know what you're talking about. We were just fine before they came. There was no risk or threat of anything."

"Now I know that you're delusional, Jeffrey. What about the threat of a third World War? And the ongoing risk of a nuclear war, and the complete annihilation of the entire human race?"

"Look, I'm not going to accept this situation. I'm not. I'm going to change things for the better. And with my experience, training, and connections it will be very easy to do so."

"How?"

"How else? I'm going to bring the army back together again. Together, we can stop this nonsense."

"Are you out of your mind, Jeffrey? What army? All armies have long been disbanded. Have you forgotten?"

"No, I haven't forgotten, but I'm going to do it anyway."

"You can't do such a thing, Jeffrey. There are no weapons anywhere, and neither are there soldiers who would join you."

"Leave that to me to worry about, Madam President. Are you going to join us?"

"Join you? In what?"

"In the offensive we are soon going to launch against the Future People."

"Are you crazy? Did you not see what happened to the protesters in London and Beijing?"

"Yes, I saw it and that's why I'm going to fight back. You have to take a stand on this, Madam President. Are you in or out?"

"Are you giving me an ultimatum?"

"I'm afraid I am, Madam President. You have to decide whose side you are on. And you have to do it quickly."

President Parker bit her lip. "This is too sudden, Jeffrey. You have to give me some time to think about it."

"Take the time you need while I go and get things ready. But remember that when the time does come, you have to declare which side you're on."

"I can't give you an answer now, Jeffrey. Let me think about it."

"Okay then, Madam. I think I'd better be going."

"When are you going to come round again?"

"Maybe next week. Make sure you have made up your mind by then."

"I'll do my best."

After Jeffrey had left, President Parker stood up and walked to one of her windows. She watched him walk out of the grounds of the White House, then disappear. She approached one of Davius' orderlies outside her bedroom. "Get me Davius immediately."

"Yes, ma'am. Right away."

Few minutes later, she handed over the phone to President Parker. "Commander Davius?"

"Yes, Madam President. How is the United States today?"

"Fine, thank you, Commander."

"I was going through your latest report. Did you want to add something to it?"

"No, this is not about the report, Commander. It's something very different."

"I see. What is it, Madam President?"

"I just got a visit from my former Defense Secretary."

"Is that so? Is there anything wrong with you being visited by a former aide?"

"Not generally, Commander. But when that person tells you that they are going to plan a revolution, then I think it is."

"A revolution? Where?"

"Right here, Commander; right here in the United States."

"I see. So your former Defense Secretary wants to jeopardize world peace by starting a revolution here in the USA?"

"Yes, he left the White House not long ago."

"Very well. Thank you for the intelligence report. I'll look into it."

"Commander? Commander Davius?"

"Yes, Madam President?"

"I'm sorry, but you don't seem alarmed. You sound very calm about what I've just told you."

Davius chuckled. "Why should I be alarmed? I know that they will fail. Anyone who plans a revolution against us will never succeed. Never. So why should I be alarmed?"

"I see. Okay then. Thank you."

"You're welcome, madam. And thank you again for the information."

CHAPTER 9

Jeffrey was a short distance away from President Parker's bedroom window. He was hiding amongst the shrubs and flower gardens that skirted the White House lawn. He had been hiding there since he left the President's bedroom. He was well aware of the current curfew that was in place. He knew that if he ventured outside the White House before sunrise, he would easily be apprehended. So, he chose to remain hidden in the grounds of the White House until it was safe to move around.

After a while, Jeffrey glanced at his wrist watch. It was already a few minutes past six. He moved stealthily like a cheetah and was able to sneak out unnoticed. Soon, just outside the White House, he was walking down the street. He flagged down a cab.

Jeffrey arrived home, took a shower had something to eat and went to bed, he needed to sleep considering that he didn't have much sleep in the last couple of days, his anxiousness and excitement to meet President Parker kept him awake.

He woke up few hours later, prepared himself a cup of coffee and a sandwich. He cleared his table and laid down new set of papers, and started writing down his plan in detail. He looked at the time; it was 2:00 pm, picked up his smartphone and dialed a number. "Hello, Bradley? Where are you right now?"

"I'm on my way to the gym."

"I see. I'd like to see you urgently."

"Urgently?"

"Yes, urgently."

"Where?"

"My place."

"Okay."

"Could you get Martins to come with you too?"

"Martins? You want both of us to come to your place?"

"Yes."

"Sure, I'll go fetch Martins and we'll come straight to you. I guess we can skip the gym today."

"Great. Looking forward to seeing you."

Soon, the three men were together in Jeffery's house.

"I'm glad you could make it at such short notice."

"We wouldn't dream of ignoring a call from you, Mr. Secretary," Martins replied.

"Please, don't. I'm no longer the Defense Secretary, just call me Jeffrey. There is something very important to discuss and plan before briefing the others."

Bradley frowned. "Briefing the others? Who are you referring to?"

"I'm referring to our most dedicated and trustworthy officers," Jeffrey said. "Surely, you must have some dedicated officers who you can still contact?"

Bradley nodded. "Yes, absolutely."

"What's this all about?" Martins asked.

"I just met with the president."

"President Parker?" Bradley asked.

"Yes, the original one I hope. But then again, I'm not too sure. These days, I don't even know what's real or fake anymore. Anyway, I met with her to tell her of my suspicions about what's going on. You are all aware of what these so-called Future People did to the people in Beijing and London, right?"

The two men nodded.

"Well, contrary to what the world thinks, I don't think that they were taken to some fancy planet somewhere in space. I believe that they were all killed, murdered in cold blood, by the Future People."

Bradley blinked. "Are you serious?"

"I couldn't be more serious. Look, I know what I'm saying. The Future People are out to annihilate the present-day human race. They want to completely obliterate us. And we simply cannot allow it."

"So what do you propose we do? They're in charge, aren't they?" Martins asked.

"No, they aren't," Jeffrey said. "*We* are the ones in charge. *We* are the ones that will force a change of situation for the better."

"What do you have in mind?" Martins asked.

"You are both senior Generals, aren't you?" The two men nodded. "Good. And that means that in spite of the worldwide clamp-down, dismantling, and disengagement of armies and army personnel, you are men who still command tremendous respect from your former troops, am I right?" Again the two men nodded.

"Perfect," Jeffrey said. "What I'm proposing is that we lead a select number of our trusted military men and women against the Future People; force them to surrender and relinquish power back to us."

"You mean like a revolution?" Martins asked.

"No, more like a coup than a revolution."

"That's going to be quite risky, you know?" Bradley said. "After Beijing and London, the Future People are now more alert than ever before. They will easily detect any new movements."

"And that's where we will need to be more discrete and strategic," Jeffrey said. "The Beijing and London incidents weren't manned by experienced and well-trained military strategists, professionals, and tacticians like us. They were simply the inevitable outcome of some poor planning and weak organization by frustrated, ordinary citizens. But that will never happen to us. Why? Because we are Generals, high-ranking officers who know how to get large scale operations done with minimum risk but maximum damage."

"So you think a coup here in the US is the solution?" Bradley asked.

"It's the only way out of this mess humanity has found itself in. And I'm sure of it, because their mothership has remained stationed here. They could have decided to put it elsewhere but they chose the US—or rather, New York, to be precise. If we execute our plan very well, we should be able to take over their mothership. And as in any conflict, once the headquarters of the enemy is defeated, the battle is as good as won."

Bradley nodded. "Yes, you're right about that, Jeffrey. Once we get a hold of their mothership, we will get a firm grip on them. But we will need time to prepare and strategize."

"Yes, I know. We will take our time to perfect everything. There's no hurry here."

"You made mention of going to the White House to see the President," Martins asked.

"Yes, I did. I met with President Parker."

"Did you tell her your plan?"

"Yes, I did."

"Is she in support of it?" Martins asked.

"She said she needed time to consider it."

"She needs time?" Martins asked. "But what is there to consider?"

"She's the President. Maybe she doesn't want to be rushed into such things." Jeffrey replied.

"But it's not as if you need her support for anything," Martins pointed out. "I mean, what support can she really give anyway, she's just a figurehead doing Davius' bidding? It's not as if she has any power or authority of her own."

"So, what are you saying?" Jeffrey asked.

"I'm saying maybe you shouldn't have gone to see her in the first place. She is Davius' stooge, and so are all the other world leaders right now. I think for the time being you have to avoid her," Martins said.

"You think she might rat us out to Davius?" Jeffrey asked.

Martins nodded. "She might already have done so—that is, if she is that loyal to Davius. And from what I understand, all heads of state are fiercely loyal to him."

"Fiercely loyal to him? No wonder she couldn't see any sense or reason in my suspicions."

"Anyway, let's not worry about what we can't control," Martins said. "I think we should focus our energies on what we *can* control, which is the outcome of this coup."

"Alright," Jeffrey nodded. "So what are your initial thoughts about this?"

Bradley sat up. "Well, I think your idea is doable. And not just doable, but we can almost certainly succeed—because you're right, we aren't some rag-tag pack of angry, ordinary citizens without any clear focus or experience. We are military men and well-trained for this sort of thing."

Jeffrey nodded. "Exactly my thoughts."

"Okay, so how many people would we need to carry out this operation?" Martins asked.

"Twenty thousand would do the job," Jeffrey said.

"Twenty?" Martins asked. "Twenty thousand?"

Jeffrey nodded. "Yes, that's what we would need, since we need to take care of any armed Future People that might want to get in our way. We need at least twenty thousand soldiers who would do anything to salvage our country and the world from this madness."

"You really think we can get that many people to support our cause, who we can trust?" Martins asked.

"Yes, of course we can. You don't think that just because Davius has dismantled the army and everything military, there are therefore no men and women who would fight for their country, do you?" Jeffrey said.

"Well, I know there would still be some somewhere, but I never thought it would be as high as twenty thousand," Martins confessed.

"There are at least that many out there, I'm sure of it." Jeffrey insisted. "And we're going to need every single one of them."

"So, what else do we need to consider?" Martins asked.

"Our major points of attack and influence," Bradley said. "For now, if you ask me, our major focus point has to be the mothership. I mean, that's where everything is being run, isn't it? If we can take over command of that ship then, we can take over command of Planet Earth."

"I agree, but we need to be very organized about this. Moving twenty thousand soldiers to New York is bound to raise a lot of attention," Martins said.

"Not if there is a reason for that many people to be there in the first place," Bradley offered. "Don't we still have festivals or something similar in New York these days?"

Jeffrey picked up a newspaper on the table next to them and flipped it open. "I can see some games lined up for the weekends ahead—football and basketball. There are also concerts, plays and museum exhibitions on the weekend, during daylight hours."

"So, we have a reason for New York to accommodate as many as twenty thousand troops of ours," Martins said. "Though in order to be discrete, they need to get to New York individually, never en masse. They need to come in one after the other, all dressed in their usual civilian wear."

Bradley nodded. "Yes, and they would need to use different routes—they can go by train, bus and even plane. No two troops would be on the same flight or other means of transport at the same time."

"You're right," Martins agreed. "Luckily, New York is a big state and there are always multiple trips in and out, every single hour of a day. As much as possible, they also need to avoid staying in the same buildings, or at least the same hotel floors."

"Can we control accommodation like that?" Jeffrey asked. "We also need them to be within close range so that we can easily assemble, without having to wait for some to come from very far away."

"I think you have a point there," Bradley agreed. "We need to have everyone close by so that we can assemble with little notice. I think we might have to allow them to stay on the same floors of hotels and buildings; it might be inevitable to make sure our plan works. But we could still instruct them to avoid each other and to never discuss the mission details with each other."

"Yes, a strict code of silence needs to be maintained by everyone at all times," Martins said. "Now, how about logistics and communication? And beyond that, how do we relay decisions, tactics, and plans to such a large number of personnel?"

"You mean without getting the attention of Davius' intelligence network? I think I have an idea. Their network is simply that—a network. We can bypass the known channels of communication and install our own protocols."

"How would you do that, Jeffrey? It's not as if we can set up our own network," Martins pointed out.

"No, we aren't setting up anything new. Have you forgotten that back in the Pentagon we had a series of channels that were available for communication between us and those on the field?" Jeffrey asked.

Bradley snapped his fingers. "Yes, yes, you're right! We used those channels for contacting our troops in Afghanistan, Iraq, and Syria. They were very secure channels that bypassed the usual communication channels that everyone else was using. But weren't they decommissioned when all the military and army structures were dismantled?"

"Yes, they were, but I still have the access codes and integration keys. They may have dismantled the structures, but that doesn't mean that they completely destroyed everything." Jeffrey replied.

"Then we don't have any problem with communications," Martins said.

"No, not at all. We can easily get a good tech guy from one of our loyal personnel to run the protocol using a tough shield that would mask our communication," Jeffrey said. "It would be like a parasite on the existing communications framework that the Future People are already monitoring—except that they would never be able to detect *our* signals."

***

They continued to discuss their plan, until Jeffrey glanced at his wall clock. "It's almost five already," he observed. "I think we should call it a day for now. We will continue tomorrow."

Bradley nodded. "Yeah, you're right. The curfew starts at six. Martins and I need to leave right now to make sure we get home on time."

CHAPTER 10

Just as they were about to disperse, there was a knock on the door. They all froze and exchanged glances. "Are you expecting anyone?" Bradley asked Jeffrey.

Jeffrey shook his head. "No."

"And even if he was, would they really show up right before the start of the curfew?" Martins wondered aloud.

Jeffrey shook his head. "Either way, I'm not expecting anyone at all."

The knock came again.

Jeffrey frowned. "Who is it?" he called out.

"Please open up, Mr. Watson. We need to talk with you immediately," came the response.

"We?" Jeffrey repeated. "Who are you?"

"The patrol team responsible for this area."

Jeffrey's mouth dropped open. He glanced at the others. "The patrol team?" he whispered.

"We also need to talk with your colleagues in there with you," the voice continued.

Bradley exchanged glances with the others. "They know we're here?"

"Are you going to open up or do you want us to break down your door?"

"No, don't," Jeffrey said, walking towards the door. "Just hold on. I'll open it now."

As soon as he opened the door, four heavily-armed Future People rushed into his house. They were holding automatic laser rifles whose barrels were glowing red. Jeffrey and the other two stood still with their hands in the air. They knew what the red barrels represented—the safety catches of the laser guns were off, which meant that the soldiers were ready to fire at the slightest provocation.

One of the Future People stepped forward from the crowd to walk up to Jeffrey. As she approached, Jeffrey and his colleagues fell silent.

She stopped directly in front of Jeffrey and glanced at the other two. "How are we today, gentlemen?"

"We're doing just fine, officer," Jeffrey said. "Why do you ask? And why are you here in my house?"

"Well, no reason, really. But we couldn't help but notice that since your friends arrived to your house, you have all remained sitting in the same room. We were wondering if there is a problem."

Jeffrey shook his head. "I don't understand, officer. Is any law being broken when friends gather together to have a drink in a private house like this?"

"Not really. Except maybe if they are planning on breaking laws."

Jeffrey exchanged glances with his colleagues. "Planning on breaking laws? Excuse me, but I don't understand what you're talking about here. Can you be more explicit?"

"You visited the President last night, didn't you?"

"Officer, can you please tell me what this is all about?"

"I'm just telling you that we have our eyes on everyone who might pose a threat."

"A threat to what? Do you realize that I served this country at the highest level possible? How can I be a threat?"

"I'm just saying, Mr. Watson, you can never be sure. People change, you know?"

"No, I don't know. Perhaps you might be able to enlighten me?"

"You think we don't know what you're up to, Mr. Watson? You think we don't already know everything that you and your friends have been discussing since you all met here?"

"Excuse me, but what wrong have we done by meeting together like this?"

"What wrong?" the officer asked. She took out a device and turned it on. As she did, an audio recording began to play back. On it, Jeffrey, Bradley, and Martins' voices could be heard clearly talking. It was a short clip of some of the things that they had been talking about not so long ago.

Martins gasped, while Bradley dropped his hands involuntarily as they both fell to their knees. Only Jeffrey remained standing with his hands still raised. He only shook his head in disdain.

"This is the audio recording of all your conversations today. We have the video as well."

"You're mistaken. We are simply ordinary citizens."

The officer nodded and raised her laser rifle. "Yes, ordinary citizens who have an extraordinary agenda. You are all under arrest."

The others raised their hands in the air and remained silent, but Jeffrey continued to protest. "You can't arrest us just like that. We know our rights. We haven't done anything wrong."

The officer pointed her gun at Jeffrey. "You must love delusional thinking, Mr. Watson. You can keep on dreaming, but you're all coming with us. Now move, or else we will be forced to use every available means to move you."

Jeffrey shook his head as each of their wrists was snapped into handcuffs. They were then led outside the house. Once outside, they were all bundled into a spacecraft that had landed on the street just outside Jeffrey's house. Some of the neighbors were peeping at them through their windows. No one dared to come out and see what was happening. Apart from the fear of confronting the invading soldiers, the curfew was already in effect. Anyone caught outside at that moment would be arrested and detained for questioning and prosecution.

As the spacecraft readied for takeoff, Jeffrey put his head in his hands and groaned. "How did this happen? How could they have known?"

"The President must have reported you to Davius," Martins said.

Jeffrey shook his head. He clenched his fists. "How could she do this to me? I was her Defense Secretary!"

"That was in the past. Have you forgotten that she now has someone she reports to?" Martins pointed out.

"I should've known. My God, I really should've known that her loyalty was no longer with her country, but with Davius and the Future People."

His mind was as numb as his body was weak. He didn't know what to think at that moment. His thoughts were racing past him like bullets erratically shooting out of the barrel of a machine gun. He couldn't keep his mind on anything as his eyes darted around. The armed Future People were watching him, their guns still pointed at him. Jeffrey wondered what could be going through their minds as they watched him.

He sighed and glanced outside the window. He couldn't imagine what their fate would be. *What will happen to us?* He wondered.

Jeffrey couldn't believe that his plan had suddenly blown up in his face. He wasn't just staring at his failure to execute a coup, but also the imminent threat of their execution.

There was no doubt in his mind that he and his colleagues were all going to die, executed for believing in their freedom.

Is this how my life is going to come to an end? he wondered.

Is this how I'm going to die?

Am I going to be responsible for the death of these two fine soldiers?

What have I done?

What was I thinking?

How could I've thought it would be possible to overpower the troops from the future?

With what, outdated ammunition and technology?

Jeffrey shook his head and sighed.

I've made a terrible mistake. And now that mistake is going to lead us to our deaths.

The spaceship began to lift off, flying vertically into the sky. A short while later, it began to fly horizontally, zooming past several familiar buildings that were dotted across the landscape below.

CHAPTER 11

The spaceship soon docked into one side of the mothership. As it did, Jeffrey couldn't help but appreciate the sheer size of the mothership. Compared to the first spaceship, it was as if an insect had nestled itself into the trunk of a tree.

Inside, the spaceship flew through a huge tunnel before landing. Jeffrey looked outside and was completely taken aback by what he saw. They were now in an enormous holding facility where other spaceships were also parked.

While Jeffrey was still admiring the view of the mothership, he heard footsteps approaching. Soon, there were several armed officers in front of them.

Jeffrey, Bradley and Martins were led out of the spaceship into a larger hall. After waiting for a while, a door opened and some armed Future People walked into the hall. They were escorting someone.

"Maybe it's another one of us they are bringing in?" Bradley suggested.

"No, it's not one of us," Jeffrey replied. "It's him. It's Davius."

All of them watched closely as Davius walked to the front. His hands were clasped behind his back as he walked across the room and stood in front of them.

"My fellow people of Earth," Davius said. "Jeffrey, Bradley, and Martins, I cannot begin to express how disappointed I am in you."

As Davius spoke, there were drones flying all around him. They had cameras mounted on them. Even before the walls of the hall turned into huge flat screens with their footage streaming live, the three men knew that they were already on televisions, computers and mobile devices all over the world.

"But even though I'm deeply disappointed in you three, that doesn't mean that I'm disappointed in the entire human race. No, that isn't the case. Because for me to say so means that, I don't see any future for our race. And we all have a great future. Yes, we do! It's a future that I've seen, one that I've been to. One that I will do everything in my power to preserve and ensure that you in this present day will live to see too."

Davius turned at this moment to look into the camera of a drone that was hovering very close to him. His image was amplified on the widescreens on the walls of the hall. "Fellow people around the world, just few hours ago, we were able to stop a revolution that might have occurred in the United States."

Davius pointed behind him and the camera zoomed into the faces of the three men. "Can you believe that these men didn't want to abide by our rules and regulations? They didn't want peace and order to reign on Earth."

The cameras focused on the handcuffed men for a moment, before focusing back on Davius.

"I said I wasn't disappointed by humanity, because we are all part and parcel of that humanity—whether we are from the future or, like you, from the present. We sent away the Chinese dissidents to Planet Xanadu for life sentences. The English are going to serve harsh and difficult life sentences on the same planet. And for these three, these American rebels, we are going to deal with them in an equally harsh way as well."

Jeffrey shook his head. "This is all my fault," he said quietly. "But what we were fighting for was noble, just, and true. It was."

Bradley nudged him to keep quiet. Jeffrey obeyed.

"Fellow people of this present time, these American rebels would have completely eradicated my administration. But that was if they had been successful. Unfortunately for them, they were not. What truly upsets me though, is the caliber of people behind the revolution.

"People of former repute. People like the former Defense Secretary of the United States and some of his former top Generals. Now tell me this, did they think that they could pull off such an audacious mission without me knowing? Didn't they realize that our intelligence and surveillance systems are incredibly advanced?"

Jeffrey noticed Martins glaring at him. He looked away, not bothering to engage. He knew what Martins was thinking at that very moment: *I told you so.*

"We will ship these dissidents to Planet Xanadu. I implore all of present-day humanity to take this as another lesson. In fact, not just another lesson, but the third example of what we will do to anyone in any part of the world who tries to stand up to our authority and power."

As Davius completed the broadcast, Jeffrey shouted. "You're not going to get away with this!"

Some of the Future People raised their weapons at Jeffrey. But Davius signaled to them and they lowered their weapons immediately. "What am I not going to get away with, Mr. Watson?" Davius asked him calmly.

"The mass murder of the people of Planet Earth, of course," Jeffrey spat. "You think I don't know the truth? You think that we don't already know the truth? That you're simply exterminating the people of present-day Earth, one group after the other? You think we don't already know this?"

Davius raised his eyebrows. "Extermination? Where? How?"

"On that planet of yours, of course. First you killed the Chinese, then you did the same to the English. Now you're going to do the same to us."

Davius shook his head. "My, my, my. And what's giving you all these ideas? Where did you get all this false information from?"

"I don't need to get the information from anywhere," Jeffrey scoffed. "The evidence is there for anyone wise enough to see. You are only here to exterminate present-day humans, and nothing more."

Davius nodded. "I see. Okay, then in that case you might need to be re-educated on your way to Planet Xanadu."

"What sort of re-education are you talking about? I know you're going to kill me, as well as the rest of us!" Jeffrey spat.

"That's where you're very wrong, Mr. Watson. You will soon find out," Davius said then turned to some of his troops. "Load them all up and commence their immediate evacuation to Planet Xanadu."

"You're not going to get away with this!" Jeffrey shouted again, as he and the others were being led away. But Davius didn't respond this time. With his hands still behind his back, he walked out of the hall, accompanied by his orderlies.

The three men were led to another facility containing several spaceships of the same design. Jeffrey noticed that these spaceships were quite different from the one that had brought them from Washington to the mothership. They were much larger and wider. A troop of armed Future People led them into one of the spaceships. Inside, there were several seats. They all sat down. Soon, the three men were freed of their handcuffs and offered refreshments.

Jeffrey turned to his colleagues. "These must be transporters. They are going to transport us to somewhere unknown so they can kill us."

"But why would they waste resources on killing us?" Martins asked. "Why wouldn't they just do it here on Earth?"

"And let the people see their true intentions?" Jeffrey asked. "You think they would expose themselves?"

"It just doesn't make any sense," Martins said. "Why would they do that?"

No one responded to Martins' question. Several Future People were walking around them with their guns. They eventually all settled in reserved seats in different parts of the spaceship.

Jeffrey saw some of the other spaceships taking off, flying out of the mothership. Jeffrey noticed that even though their spaceship must have been large enough to accommodate its many passengers, it still looked so small in comparison to the mothership.

Their spaceship was heading skywards towards the clouds. Soon, they were above them. They continued to head upwards until they left the Earth's atmosphere and began to fly through space.

"Maybe they just want to dump us out here in space," Jeffrey suggested.

"And litter space with our bodies?" Martins wondered. "Don't you think people would notice dead bodies floating around space, even from Earth?"

Jeffrey shook his head as he looked outside the window close to him. "Would you see a body in all this darkness out here? Tell me, would you?"

"You would, if you looked hard enough," Martins said. "We can see stars from Earth, can't we? Even the moon is clearly visible. Abandoned bodies wouldn't be a hard thing to spot with a powerful telescope."

"They're going to kill us. Who has ever heard of any planet called Xanadu? I'm sure it doesn't exist."

"Just because we haven't heard of it doesn't mean that it doesn't exist, Jeffrey," Martins replied.

"Maybe it's just part of their ploy to deceive us all. Planet Xanadu indeed!"

"Maybe it isn't. They *are* from the future, aren't they? So, why should their Planet Xanadu be in our own time? Clearly, the planet is not in our solar system; it might not even be in this present time."

"What kind of an explanation is that? Are you even listening to yourself, Martins? You're just taking sides and making excuses on behalf of the Future People."

"I'm not taking sides or making excuses for anyone. I'm only analyzing the facts available and making an informed judgement."

"Informed judgement, hah! Look, let me tell you, this analysis won't help us, because we're—"

"Guys! Look!" Bradley cut in.

The three men looked ahead. They could see what appeared to be a giant ring shining in the middle of the path that all the spaceships were heading for. It looked like a ring of orange and red fire, burning bright in the darkness of space.

"It's the sun," Jeffrey said. "They want to throw us into the sun!"

"Get a grip of yourself, Jeffrey!" Martins admonished. "Would they do such a thing with their own troops on board?"

"What could it be?" Bradley wondered. "It doesn't look like the sun, because the sun is a whole complete star, while this... this thing—it's like a ring burning on its own! I've never seen anything like it before."

"Attention everyone on board," an electronic voice announced. "We are about to transit through the portal. Please remain seated and stay calm. Thank you."

"Portal? What portal?" Jeffrey asked.

But he didn't have time to think. The spaceships headed for the portal. It was incredibly wide and could fit more than a hundred spaceships flying side by side.

The three men had been allowed to move freely on the ship until now, but at that moment, one of the officers beckoned to them. "You have to take your seats now and fasten your seatbelts. We are about to go through the portal."

As their spaceship flew into the portal, Jeffrey gasped. It was as if they had walked through a doorway that connected a very dark room to one that was filled with light.

The transformation was sudden and drastic. One moment they were in the deep darkness of space, racing towards the fiery ring, and the next they were surrounded by bright lights. The portal was like an enormous tunnel; moving through it reminded Jeffrey of travelling on a high-speed train through an underground tunnel back on Earth.

But unlike the train tunnels on Earth that were usually lit with white and yellow light bulbs, the lights inside the portal were all the colors of the rainbow. Jeffrey didn't only see white and yellow lights, but also red, blue, purple, orange, and so many other colors that he couldn't easily identify them all. And rather than the sort of lights Jeffrey associated with train tunnels, these lights were being reflected by strange shapes in the portal. As Jeffrey stared at the wonderful display of lights, he felt like he was now inside a colorful tube and not a speed tunnel—or even a portal for that matter.

Martins was now pointing. "Look! Can you see how fast we're moving?"

Bradley shook his head. "For those colors to be static and easily identifiable by us while we are inside a spaceship of this size, we must be moving at a tremendous speed. Perhaps several times the speed of light!"

Jeffrey nodded. "Yes, you're absolutely right! We're travelling faster than the speed of light."

CHAPTER 12

No one said anything else throughout the remainder of the trip. Jeffrey couldn't tell how long their trip lasted.

Eventually, he looked out of one of the windows and noticed that the spaceship was no longer flying through the pitch black of outer space. They were now flying over vast amount of water.

"Transit through the portal has been successful," the same electronic voice said. "We have safely arrived on Planet Xanadu."

"Planet Xanadu?" Jeffrey repeated. "These people think we are fools. They just took us on a round trip and brought us back to Earth."

"How can you say we are on Earth?" Martins wondered. "We left Earth behind us to head to the portal that was in front of us. And once we went through it, we left Earth far behind."

"We are on Earth," Jeffrey insisted. "We *must* be on Earth!"

"Jeffrey," Bradley said. "I don't think this is Earth."

"These blue waters," Jeffrey said. "we are flying over one of Earth's oceans."

Bradley frowned. "No, we're not. Blue waters do not mean we are still on Earth."

"But more importantly," Martins said. "If we are on Earth as Jeffrey is insisting, then that means that they want to kill us on Earth, doesn't it? Why take us on a round trip through space then back to Earth, just to kill us? Why?"

Jeffrey didn't say anything. He couldn't say anything. He was busy thinking. *Where could we be? What's going to happen to us here?*

The spaceship continued to fly over the ocean then reached what seemed to be an island in the middle of the ocean or a continent because of its size. The spaceship started descending and heading towards what appeared to be an inhabited area filled with buildings, and towering structures. The scenery was beautiful with lots of expansive green gardens around. The buildings and edifices were sleek and well-designed.

All around, they could see modern structures. There were tall skyscrapers, smaller buildings, and several other interesting structures. None of them looked familiar.

"Where is this place?" Jeffrey asked no one in particular as they flew above the buildings. The vegetation was lush with rich, long, green leaves. The stones were polished and seemed to shine, even from the height at which they were flying. The buildings seemed to be made of pure crystal glass. There were some tall, imposing ones while others were smaller like bungalows with shiny domes.

Once the spaceship had landed, the armed Future People stood up and began to lead the passengers off the spaceship. Jeffrey and the two generals were the first to be walked out on metallic gangways.

Outside, they saw several large buildings in the form of multi-story apartments.

The three men were led to a separate wing of apartments. After walking through a series of gates, the soldiers opened the door to an apartment.

"What's going on?" Jeffrey asked one of the soldiers as they went inside.

"You're now in your prison apartment," the soldier said.

"Prison apartment? When are we going to be killed?" Jeffrey asked.

The soldier shook his head. "You aren't going to be killed. You're going to stay in the prison apartment and serve out your prison term."

"Wait, are you saying that this isn't Earth?" Jeffrey asked.

"Earth? We left Earth a long time ago," the soldier said. "You don't expect us to imprison you on Earth, do you? Your prison facilities on Earth are severely outdated and antiquated."

"Outdated and antiquated?" Jeffrey repeated. "You don't know what you're talking about. You can't reduce us to nothing just like that. We've made great advancements in most areas of human endeavors!"

Bradley tugged at Jeffrey's sleeve. "Stop arguing and look."

Jeffrey glanced out the window where Bradley was pointing. It looked like a wide field with soft, well-cut green grass. There were some people walking around there.

Jeffrey frowned as he watched them. "Are those–"

"The protesters," Bradley finished.

Jeffrey shook his head. "No, I don't believe this."

"Why don't we go and find out ourselves?" Bradley suggested.

Jeffrey turned to one of the soldiers with them. "Are we...can we..."

"You want to go and join the others in the recreation fields?" the soldier asked. "Of course you can. Feel free to move around anywhere within this prison facility."

The three men hurried to the fields outside. Once they got there, Jeffrey approached one of them. "Excuse me, are you a human being?"

The woman chuckled at him. "Yes, I'm a human being. What about you, are you also a human being?"

Jeffrey nodded. "Yes, I am. When did you come here?"

"Me, or rather we—my entire group—we arrived few months ago," the woman said.

"Did you meet anyone here when you came?" Bradley asked.

The woman nodded. "Yes, of course. The Chinese were here before us."

"The Chinese?" Jeffrey repeated. "Wait, you mean to say that you are—"

The woman nodded. "Yes, I'm from London."

Jeffrey gasped. "No way!"

The woman frowned at him. "Why? You seem surprised."

"But I thought, I thought—I thought you were killed, all of you!" Jeffrey exclaimed.

The woman laughed. "Killed? Didn't you listen to the broadcast that Davius made when we were all rounded up? He said we were going to be imprisoned in facilities on Planet Xanadu. Well, here we are."

"You mean we aren't on Earth?" Jeffrey asked.

"Earth? No, this is Planet Xanadu, not Earth!"

Jeffrey glanced at Bradley. "Can you believe this? They weren't killed!"

"Wait, it seems like you are all new here," the woman observed. "Where are you from anyway?"

"Us? We're from the USA," Jeffrey said.

"Really? So it was true after all?" the woman said.

"What was true?" Jeffrey asked.

"We saw the broadcast that Davius made a while ago, about a revolution that had been quelled in the US. We just didn't think it could be possible. I mean, how could anyone still think of revolting against these Future People? So it *was* true? You *did* try to revolt against them?"

Jeffrey sighed. "We thought your group of London rebels had been killed along with the Chinese dissidents. That's why we wanted to revolt."

"We've just been here the whole time," the woman replied.

Jeffrey bit his lip and slapped his forehead. "What a fool I've been! What have I done?"

Bradley held his shoulder and patted him. "Calm down, Jeffrey. It wasn't your fault."

"Of course it's my fault," Jeffrey said as he looked around. He could see some more of the protesters from Beijing and London. "This is all my fault. I shouldn't have been so stupid and acted on my suspicions. No one was killed. Everyone is alive and safe here."

"I told you, didn't I?" Martins said.

***

That night, Jeffrey couldn't sleep, he couldn't stop thinking

I was stupid, so very stupid. I was completely wrong. The Future People aren't liars. They aren't murderers. They were really honest about their intentions towards us. They want to

ensure world peace and order, yet there I was fighting them. How stupid I've been. How stupid of me!

CHAPTER 13

A week later, Davius was getting ready to make an announcement. The people of Earth were rapt as he appeared on their screens. "Fellow people of Planet Earth," he said. "With effect from today, I am pleased to announce that the curfew has been lifted all across the planet. In addition to that, all communication channels, media, and the Internet have been released back to you all to use as you deem fit. Thank you."

In major cities around the world, there were tremendous celebrations. Everyone was excited and happy as they began to live their lives again in a free and peaceful way.

***

A few days later, Davius appeared once again to make another announcement. "Fellow people of this good planet Earth, I greet you all. I would like to use this opportunity to announce that we are offering a one-week tourist package to our Planet Xanadu at the cost of only one hundred dollars per person. This trip will comprise full board and accommodation, and is open to every one of you. The money from this initiative will be utilized to provide clean water projects here on Earth. I encourage you all to take this opportunity. By doing so, you will not only have the opportunity of visiting the beautiful and advanced Planet Xanadu, but you would also assist in providing clean water projects for your Planet Earth."

A lot of people were very excited with the announcement; the number of registrations was unprecedented. People signed up for the tourist trip in their thousands. Those who were the first to take part came back with fantastic stories and rave reviews about Planet Xanadu. When they returned home, they were gushing about how wonderful both the trip and the planet had been. According to them, Planet Xanadu was twenty times bigger than Earth. It had beautiful parks and beaches, colorful trees and elegant buildings. They described the advanced technologies, the hovering vehicles and the sidewalks which moved like conveyor belts, taking the pedestrians to wherever they wanted to go.

The people of Earth who were able to go found themselves learning about the Xanadu way of life and experiencing their peaceful lifestyles firsthand. They also praised how safe the planet is and how everyone enjoyed equal opportunities, equality and fairness in every aspect.

That increased the urge for those who had not yet booked their trips to apply quickly, while people who had already booked waited anxiously for their turn to embark on the trip.

The second batch of tourists discovered that the planet was everything its name had suggested it might be. In terms of size, Planet Xanadu was indeed twenty times larger than Earth. It had almost perfect, lush vegetation, with beautiful trees and colorful flowers. Its beaches were clean and inviting, and so were its clear blue waters. The buildings in its cities and residential areas were neat and ultra-modern.

Even though the technology in place was very advanced and covered almost every aspect of life there, it was all extremely user-friendly and adaptable, such that the present-day people found it easy to grasp how to use it.

In addition to technological advancements, the tourists also discovered state-of-the-art entertainment facilities such as cinemas, casinos, strip clubs, and recreational parks. Above all, the people there were extremely friendly, warm, and hospitable. The tourists also discovered that food and accommodation on the planet were entirely free of charge. The lifestyle and ways of the people on Planet Xanadu were extremely peaceful and calm, unlike anything any person from Earth had ever seen before or even imagined.

***

"The feedback seems to have caused an increase in our registrations," observed one of Davius' deputies, a few days later. "A lot of people have been rushing to make more bookings, while those who have previously been there are rebooking for another week-long vacation."

"Really?" Davius asked as he reviewed the report she had brought to him. "Did you say that tourists who have already been there are trying to book a second trip?"

"Yes Commander."

"But that means that they would be preventing the first-timers from going."

"Yes, that would have been the case, Commander, had our system not detected the trend. What we are now doing is giving first-timers priority."

Davius nodded. "That's better."

"But even disregarding any rebooking, the amount of first-time bookings is unbelievably high."

"Have we had any delays to any of the scheduled departures?"

"No, not at all, Commander. Not even once. Everything has been moving smoothly."

"That's great! Do keep me posted on all developments with this tourism program."

***

Three months later, Davius was in attendance at the Council Meeting to brief them of the project's success so far.

"We have been getting your reports," one member of the Council told him. "But we wanted to hear from you in person because, to say the least, the figures here are beyond impressive; they are mind-blowing."

Davius nodded. "Yes, they are. When they began to trickle in, I had to personally do an audit of our booking and reservation systems just to ensure that there was no glitch. It's not as if I doubted the effectiveness of our systems and technology, but I still wanted to be doubly sure. Even with the unexpected influx of tourists, we have perfectly maintained scheduled departures and arrivals, and we are going to keep it that way."

"Wonderful!" another Council member exclaimed. "I can also see that the news has spread to virtually every nook and cranny of Earth, so everyone is aware of the vacation opportunity."

"Yes, Council Member," Davius said. "In spite of the extensive reservations we are recording, we are still continuing with the campaign and promotion. We want to keep the news fresh in everyone's minds. And our strategy is yielding the desired results. People everywhere are talking in genuine excitement about their experiences on Planet Xanadu."

"Is that so?" another Council Member asked.

"Absolutely, Councilor. I can confidently inform this Council that as of now, Earth's definition of a luxury trip is a trip to Planet Xanadu. Do you know that nine out of ten people consider Planet Xanadu a must-see vacation destination?"

"A must-see vacation destination?" the first Council Member asked. "What about other destinations on Earth?"

Davius pointed at the widescreen in the Council Meeting briefing room. A slide appeared on it. Then another, and another. Most of them contained graphs and charts. "This data is pulled from the reports I've been generating and forwarding to you all. This shows the trend that while reservations are increasing for trips to Planet Xanadu, numbers are actually falling across all other vacation destinations on Earth."

"*All* of Earth?" the same Council Member repeated.

"Yes, Madam Councilor. In other words, people are no longer too enthralled by visiting Earth's monuments, beaches, or tourist attractions."

"Including the Eiffel Tower in France?" she asked.

"Especially the Eiffel Tower in France. The fact is, Madam Councilor, the great majority of human beings no longer regard any vacation on Earth as a vacation, when compared with a trip to Planet Xanadu."

"Well, what can we say but well done, Commander," another Council Member said. "You have recorded astounding results with the implementation of Phase B of our agenda. The human beings of this present-day Earth can now see all that Planet Xanadu is and what it can offer them."

"Thank you, Mr. Councilor," Davius bowed his head.

"You can now move onto the final phase of our agenda, Phase C," the first Council Member instructed.

"I will do that, effective immediately," Davius said.

CHAPTER 14

After he had left the meeting room, Davius went to his office. He updated his deputies, then asked them to set up the transmission and broadcast facilities so he could make another broadcast.

***

President Parker was in her office when she saw her widescreen television blink and come to life. She turned to one of the two orderlies who were always in her presence. "What's going on now?"

"It's our Commander, Madam President," one of them replied. "Commander Davius wants to make a broadcast to everyone."

President Parker remained in her seat as she paid attention to what Davius was about to say.

"Fellow men and women of this wonderful Planet Earth," Davius said. "I'm excited to be making this broadcast to you all today. On behalf of the Council, we would like to thank each and every one of you for making a vacation on Planet Xanadu the most sought-after trip that one can take."

Davius paused, as if he was expecting to hear people cheering and clapping. President Parker smiled. She couldn't help but admit that Davius was a good presenter.

"As of now, a trip to Planet Xanadu is more highly-regarded than a trip to any of the many wonderful vacation spots on Earth. All over Earth, destinations and attractions that were once highly-regarded and incredibly popular are experiencing very low patronage, and sometimes none at all. And we can only thank you all for making this happen.

"There has been an increased interest and influx of tourists to Planet Xanadu, as many of you want to keep going back again and again. Of course, we welcome repeat visitors. But if we were to allow every one of you to repeat your trips as soon as you wanted to, then we would be denying any first-timers the opportunity to experience the many beauties of Planet Xanadu."

Davius paused again and smiled, as the camera started streaming live images of happy tourists on Planet Xanadu. "We want all of you to continue to experience the joys and magic of Planet Xanadu. We don't want to restrict anyone from going there, whether they choose to visit it once, twice, or two hundred times. This is why it gives me tremendous pleasure to inform you all that effective today, any one of you who is interested in immigrating from Earth to Planet Xanadu permanently can indicate their interest to do so.

"However, eligibility is restricted to adults between the ages of 20 and 50. Apart from unlimited job opportunities, you would have free housing, free medical cover and free food too. The time limit for anyone to indicate interest in this immigration program is one month, starting today."

"What?" President Parker asked. "What is this?"

"Most of you, if not all of you, have already experienced the wonders, joy, and magic of Planet Xanadu for one week," Davius continued. "Now you have the opportunity to experience it for a lifetime. Go ahead and submit your applications."

As soon as the broadcast ended, President Parker jumped to her feet. "This cannot be happening!" she said. "This cannot be happening!"

"Madam President, what's the matter?" asked one of the orderlies.

President Parker glared back at her. "Can't you see?"

"I can't see anything unusual, Madam."

"Get me your leader right away!" President Parker ordered. "Get me Commander Davius now!"

"You want us to summon our commander here?" the other orderly asked.

"Summon? I dare not do such a thing," President Parker said. "I meant get him on the phone for me to speak with him."

The orderly placed the call. The screen in President Parker's office came to life again. "Hello, Madam President. How are you doing today?"

"I don't think I'm doing that well, Commander."

"Really? What's wrong?"

"Your broadcast, the one you made a few minutes ago."

"You mean about the offer of immigration?"

"Yes, yes, that one."

"What's wrong with it?"

"What's wrong with it? What's wrong with it? Everything is wrong with it, Commander! Why would you offer people the chance to leave Earth forever?"

"I don't see anything wrong with that, Madam President."

"You don't? But it's completely wrong. How can you entice our people to leave Earth? Don't you know what could happen? The most productive people might leave and the planet would be left completely bare without anyone to look after it."

"Well, that would be rather unfortunate, but inevitable, don't you think? But then what can we really do? We are simply reacting to the ultimate law of demand and supply. We're giving the people out there what they want. And what they want is to immigrate to Planet Xanadu."

"But that's not fair to Planet Earth, Commander."

"I don't understand what you mean by 'fair'. Is it fair for people to keep tolerating life in a place like this when they have another option—a better option, for that matter? Besides, we all know that the main causes of all the conflicts and wars on Earth have always been over-population and scarcity of resources. Therefore, we are providing the best possible solution for these problems once and for all. And through our innovative and timely solution, Earth can be preserved for those who will remain."

"But that cannot be done. They are people of Earth."

"And who are you to prevent people from going where they want to go? They are already taking us up on the offer, Madam President."

President Parker sighed heavily. As much as she didn't like the whole idea, she knew that what Davius had just said was the truth; a lot of people had of course fallen for the offer and were rushing to move to Planet Xanadu permanently.

She was at a loss for what to say when the line went dead. Soon, her phone began to ring. She didn't pick it up because she knew who it might be; her fellow counterparts from other countries trying to reach her about the immigration offer from the Future People.

She stood up from her table and walked up to the window. The spaceship was still hovering over her lawn as usual. She turned around and glanced at the ringing phone.

"Aren't you going to take the call, Madam President?" asked one of the orderlies.

She shook her head. "Let it ring. I really don't want to speak to anyone right now."

She turned away and continued to watch the stationary spaceship that was hovering over the lawn of the White House. Her mind was lost as she began to imagine what was going to happen. *Are people really going to snap up Davius' immigration offer? Are human beings really going to abandon Earth to go and live in some strange, alien land? Are people really willing to give up everything they know for the promise of a better life somewhere so far away? Are they?*

CHAPTER 15

President Parker didn't have to wonder for long.

In the coming days and weeks, people began to sign up for the offer in their thousands. The registrations for immigration soon shot up to several millions each day. Indeed, almost every eligible human being wanted to abandon Earth. They were lining up in huge numbers outside the immigration offices. In spite of their numbers, the Future People didn't have a problem controlling the crowds because their soldiers and drones were there. Besides, all those who knew they were eligible had to behave themselves, because any unruly behavior would put them at risk of losing the opportunity to immigrate.

In the lines outside the immigration offices, the enthusiasm was infectious and far-reaching. It was no longer a simple question about wanting to relocate from an undeveloped country to a more developed country; this was the chance to leave Planet Earth, for a whole world of advanced technology and a new, improved lifestyle.

The media was reporting that it was a frenzy, something that had never been experienced on such a scale before. Prior to the immigration offer, there had been popular world events in sports and entertainment like the World Cup, the Olympics, the Oscars and the Grammys, and so forth. But the public response to those events couldn't compare to the excitement about the immigration deal that Planet Xanadu offered. The buzz it generated cut across all countries, religions, cultures, and classes.

There were immigration offices in various spots around the globe, especially in the largest and most important cities on each continent. As long as an applicant met the eligibility criteria, they were allowed to enter the immigration offices to register for the program. The Future People had amiable and cheerful staff to guide the would-be applicants through every step of the registration process.

***

A month later, Davius was in his office when he received a retina hologram message. It was from the Council.

He gestured in the air to open the hologram. *Congratulations, Commander Davius. It has been exactly thirty days since we began the immigration program and as of today almost all humans between the ages of 20 and 50 have registered and have been ferried to Planet Xanadu. Phase C of our Agenda on Earth has been a resounding success. Our entire mission on Planet Earth is now complete. It is time to leave. Commence departure proceedings immediately. Thank you.*

Davius nodded to himself, as if someone was talking to him directly. He knew what he had to do. He gestured in the air once more.

"Hello, Commander," said a female voice.

"Hello. I want you to contact the five former permanent members of the United Nations," he said.

"You mean the Heads of Government of the United States America, China, Russia, France and the United Kingdom, Commander?"

"Yes, contact them all. I would like to speak to them. Start a video conference call for me to address the five of them at the same time."

"Yes, Commander. A video conference call will be set up right away."

"Thank you. Next, contact all our troops in every country of the world. Instruct them to be on standby to return to the mothership within a time frame of twenty-four hours from now. I want all the interim commanders to be fully briefed about this withdrawal. Every soldier should be on this mothership in time for our departure."

"Yes, Commander Davius," she said. "I will relay the details to everyone right away."

Davius settled down into his office chair. He was calm as he waited for the conference video call.

Few minutes later, the female voice returned. "Commander?"

"Yes, I'm here."

"You will be live with the Heads of Government in exactly ten seconds from now."

"Thank you," Davius replied and turned to the screens on his wall. One of the black screens suddenly flickered on. As it did, an image appeared of Davius looking at himself from within his own office, as if he was looking at himself from inside a mirror because the setting was exactly the same. Then five other images appeared around his own image. They were the portrait shots of each of the five Heads of Government. Under each of their images were inscription plaques identifying each dignitary. They were all there, representing the United States of America, China, Russia, France and the United Kingdom. They were all looking at him from their respective offices in their countries.

"Good day, ladies and gentlemen."

"Good day, Commander Davius," they chorused.

"Today is a good day for all of us. And by all of us, I don't just mean you, the representatives of the strongest and most powerful nations of Planet Earth. I'm actually referring to the entire human race, humanity as we know it today. Yes, it's definitely a good day, and do you know why?"

"No, Commander Davius," President Parker said. "But I presume you're going to tell us."

"Well, today is the day that I and all the other Future People take our leave from your Planet Earth to return to our own home, Planet Xanadu."

"What?" The five heads of government cried out in unison.

"You're leaving?" the Chinese President asked.

"Yes, we're leaving your planet Earth."

"But, but, but why are you leaving? You cannot leave!" the UK Prime Minister exclaimed.

"Our mission here is complete. We are leaving."

"Wait, are you trying to tell us that the threat is over? The threat of another World War, is over for good?" President Parker asked.

"What war?" Davius asked with a calm smile.

"The Third World War, of course," President Parker replied. "The one during which we sent embryos to save present-day humanity."

"What embryos are you talking about?"

"The embryos we sent into space, Commander! The embryos that populated Planet Xanadu, so that you and the others could come from the future to save our present-day Earth?"

"Don't tell me that you believed all that nonsense, Madam President. Of course we didn't come from the future."

The others gasped and began to murmur in disbelief. Only the US President was bold enough to continue interrogating Davius. "What? What are you saying, Commander? What do you mean?"

"I mean we aren't from the future, nor did we come from the future to save your present-day Earth from a future World War; there is no such thing."

"But the video," President Parker said. "What about the video where we ordered ourselves to surrender to you and your authority so that you could take over Earth?"

"Oh Madam President, do you find it difficult to accept the truth? I wonder why this is so hard for you to understand. Look, we are simply beings living on another planet, Planet Xanadu. There are others like it too; other planets that you don't yet know about."

"How did you, how..."

"Fool you? It was simple, actually. Over the course of several years, we visited your planet in secret. After observing you and your way of life for a good time, we devised a plan for how we could take over your Earth. But we wanted to achieve this at a minimal cost and with great efficiency. No doubt that after everything that has happened, we have succeeded even beyond our initial projections. I don't need to remind you about how we got you to believe in us and hand over Earth so effortlessly, in less than a few hours.

"By the way, the video you saw was actually very easy to make using our advanced technology. I must say that you were integral to our great success. Thank you for such an easy and smooth handover."

The President was shaking her head, as if trying to shake away the reality of all the new information. "But...but...but why would you do this to us? Why, Davius?"

"Come on. Surely, you of all people should know the obvious answer to that question; for your resources, of course."

"What resources? Gold, diamonds, money? What is it that you've taken away from us?" President Parker asked.

"Oh no, no, no. We were never interested in your so-called precious resources. No, we took away the single, particular resource that you had in abundance but never bothered to appreciate."

"What? What is that?" President Parker demanded.

"People. You people. Actually you never once realized that your people are your most precious resource. Unfortunately, for reasons only known to you 'world leaders', you simply chose not to appreciate your people. You've never considered your fellow human beings, or the entire human race, as a valuable resource."

"You cannot make such a ridiculous claim, Davius!" President Parker spat. "We do value our people—their liberties, their rights, and their freedoms. We do!"

"No, you don't. Not at all, and I can prove it. You see, you kill yourselves in wars with a level of recklessness that would make any other species cringe in shock, horror and dismay. Not only that, but you ignore helpless children and allow people to die of famine and illness—all the while continuing to use your wealth to stockpile nuclear ammunition. No, you so-called word leaders never really cared about your people, the people of Earth. And it is something that my people and I thought about many times before we eventually arrived here. Perhaps it's because you had so many of them. Or perhaps, at over ten billion, you must have assumed that there were more than enough people available. And so you took them for granted; something we would never have ever imagined in our wildest nightmares. And do you know why? It's because on our planet, Planet Xanadu, in spite of our larger size and abundance of resources and lovely environment, we still value the lives of our people. This is the sole reason we want them all to have a very comfortable life, one without unnecessary and avoidable pressures and worries.

"This is why we invade planets like yours, to get the manpower to work and serve the citizens of Planet Xanadu. We do this only to make sure that the people of our planet can live a life of ease and comfort. Do you see why we consider your people to be the most precious resource?"

"No wonder you had to launch that fraudulent immigration program. You just wanted to take away all the productive people from Earth!" President Parker replied angrily.

"It wasn't fraudulent," Davius replied calmly. "Your people—the same people you didn't care about—wanted a better life on a better planet, and we simply offered it to them. What's fraudulent about that?"

"You are treacherous, Davius! How many people immigrated from Earth to your planet?" she asked.

"Over half of your population."

"My God!" she exclaimed. "What about the prisoners, the ones who were taken to your Planet Xanadu for the crimes they committed here on Earth?"

"They are working in the mines on Planet Xanadu."

President Parker frowned. "Working? You mean they have jobs there?"

"Jobs? Are you kidding me? They aren't employees, if that's what you are thinking."

"I don't understand. If they aren't employees, then what are they?"

"You still don't get it, do you? They are all slaves in our mines."

"Slaves?" President Parker gasped. "You enslaved our people?"

"They are our people, now—slaves solely charged with working in our mines."

"But what about the others? What about those who immigrated to Planet Xanadu?"

"Well, they are also working in our mines. They will all be working there for the rest of their lives."

"What? So you mean to say that you enslaved our people?"

"Call it what you want. They chose the option willingly; no one forced them to immigrate to our planet."

"But this is barbaric! So, we are now left with just children and the elderly?"

"Yes, exactly, Madam President. But all hope is not lost. We still have some plans in place for those that are going to be left behind, but our plans don't include any of the elderly. You know they are no longer productive and they can't be useful to us at all. As for the children, you should take good care of them. But you're not going to be doing that for us; no, you're going to do that for the sake of Earth. Then again, who knows? We might just come back and visit again in a few years' time to take them away, because by that time they will be much older and much more productive. It'd be best to keep an eye on them for us, and for yourselves. Now I must take my leave, so good luck with running Earth!"

"You can't—" President Parker began to say. But she was talking to herself. The image of Davius had suddenly disappeared from her screen and the communication had been disconnected.

President Parker looked around. She could no longer see the orderlies that Davius had assigned to her. She stood up and rushed to one of her windows, expecting to see the spaceship that had become a permanent feature on her lawn. But now, it was no more. It was departing; it was flying away.

Almost immediately, the screen started showing images from New York. The mothership was also departing and heading for the upper regions of the Earth's atmosphere. As it moved, several smaller spaceships could be seen entering its many holds from different parts of the world.

President Parker gasped again in shock and disbelief.

It was true. The Future People were actually leaving Earth.

CHAPTER 16

After the departure of the Future People from Earth, life became surreal. Everything that people had grown to understand had radically changed yet again. Gradually, everyone had to come to terms with the fact that the able-bodied workforce was completely gone. The impact of loss of over five billion people was obvious and clear.

Life on Earth wasn't only difficult, it was now an unimaginable and unbearable. Essential services and functions like education, manufacturing, and hospitals didn't operate anymore. There were simply no skilled or qualified staff to occupy those positions anymore, because they had all left Earth.

Some of the elderly people who had retired a long time ago decided to volunteer their services in vital sectors like hospitals and educational services. They imagined that even though they were old and weak, they could still help make up for the absence of qualified workers in those sectors.

But it was a disaster.

It was simply impossible for the elderly to do all the things that the young had been doing before. While it was easy for them to handle light and menial activities that didn't require physical strength—such as education and certain hospital services—they couldn't handle the more physically demanding roles. Activities like farming and factory work deteriorated and suffered greatly. When it came to the more mentally demanding duties like maintaining and developing advanced technologies, there was simply no one amongst the elderly who could do them.

In order to bridge the gap in such fields of human endeavor that were essential for the efficient functioning of society, children were brought in to work in factories and production facilities. To ensure that the adoption of children in work places was acceptable and implementable all over the world, and that these children were protected in the workplace, laws were passed to govern child labor. Rather than being encouraged to go to school and get an education, children were now being dragged off to work.

Unsurprisingly, the provision of essential services all over Earth began to decline until they entered a state of rapid deterioration. The world as its inhabitants had known it went backwards, sending it hundreds of years in the past. Ordinary chores that could have been performed by machines became impossible when all the power plants went out of service. People all over the world had to resort to the use of charcoal and timber to generate heat and light.

With the loss of electric power came the collapse of modern transport. Airports didn't function because there were no personnel to man the control towers, nor were there pilots to fly the airplanes. Train stations shut down too for similar reasons. Only a few taxis manned by the elderly could operate. But with time, they too stopped because there was no more fuel available once all the oil refineries had shut down.

Gradually, life began to descend into a state of anarchy and confusion. Food became scarce because there was no one to cultivate the farmlands. Where crops had already been harvested, transporting them to the towns and supermarkets became impossible as there was no one to do so. Livestock that was being reared soon became agitated and escaped since there was no one to tend to them. Many of the remaining elderly had to find a way to cultivate their own food to eat.

Life was now unbearable. With the absence of a power supply, banks ceased to operate or exist. People had to resort to trade by bartering because no one had access to cash anymore. People had to devise means to provide all previously existing services for themselves. There was no more central government or regulation. Everyone was now living by themselves and for themselves.

CHAPTER 17

Meanwhile, several million light years away in the prison facilities on Planet Xanadu, Jeffrey Watson was wiping away sweat from his forehead with the back of his hand. He was wearing an orange jumpsuit, just like the others.

He gazed around. They were in a deep pit, one that must have been as deep as forty feet or more. It was as wide as a ten football fields, and filled with quite a number of people—men and women alike—all wearing orange jumpsuits and holding either shovels or pickaxes. Every morning they get transported from the isolated island which had the prison facilities to reach the mines they are now working in. Jeffrey had noticed the huge walls surrounding the mines and the guards on top of these walls and the ones at its base.

The only way in or out of the pit was via a series of ladders that were strewn around the pits. But at the foot of each ladder were two armed guards. Above, high up on the ground were more guards. They were all armed with guns that looked like steel, metallic beams, measuring about two feet in length. They reminded Jeffrey of the batons used by athletes in relay races. But they weren't batons; they were weaponized lasers with the capacity to obliterate any prisoner in that pit in an instant. He glanced at the sleeves of his suit and sniffed. The sleeves were damp and smeared with sweat and grime. The shovel in his other hand felt heavy, so he placed it down for a while and looked around.

In the pit, the other prisoners were digging, moving aside dirt, sand, and rock with their shovels and pickaxes. On the back of their orange jumpsuits were numbers and letters. Like him, each prisoner was now identified by a code. There were no more names. The code was made up of three numbers followed by two letters.

A soldier approached him. She was dressed in a grey bodysuit and had an automatic laser rifle in her hand. "You there!" she shouted. Jeffrey knew that she was referring to him, but he pretended not to hear her. "I'm talking to you!" she called again. Still, Jeffrey didn't respond. He wiped more sweat from his face with his other sleeve and stared at the smear that it left, imagining just how dirty his face must be. Above the noise of shovels and pickaxes hitting the hard ground, Jeffrey could almost hear the soldier walking towards him with her weapon pointed at his back.

"I'm talking to you, 367AD," the woman said, prodding him in the shoulder with the nozzle of her rifle.

Jeffrey turned to look at her. "I'm sorry. Were you calling me?"

She looked at him with a frown. "Yes, I was. Why did you stop digging?"

Jeffrey showed her his sleeves. "I was tired and sweaty. The sweat was blinding me. I had to stop to wipe my face."

She glanced at his dirty sleeves. "You can always clean up during the break. Now, get back to work."

Jeffrey nodded. He picked up the shovel and began to dig again. While he dug, the soldier walked away with her back turned towards him. As he watched her, he caught sight of Bradley about twenty feet away. Bradley waved at him and pointed to the ground, before making a fist. Jeffrey understood what he was saying: *the ground is really hard here.*

Jeffrey sighed. He looked away and continued digging.

He couldn't imagine that he was so many light years away from Earth. They were deep in the farthest reaches of space. He couldn't imagine that he had once been the Defense Secretary of the United States of America, and that he was now busy working alongside other prisoners in the mines of Planet Xanadu.

Jeffrey paused again. He had noticed that the number of workers in the mines had been increasing, almost on a daily basis. On this particular day, he had come across a group of workers from Africa. He didn't stop his digging but kept a close eye on them. During lunch, he approached them.

"I'm from Earth —the USA, to be exact. Where are you from?" Jeffrey asked.

"Us?" A man looked up. "We are from Uganda."

"Uganda? Let me guess, there was a revolution in Uganda and they brought you here as punishment."

The Ugandan shook his head. "No, that isn't what happened, although I do wish it was. We are immigrants; deceived and foolish immigrants, or whatever it is that you want to call us."

"Immigrants? What are you talking about?"

"The immigration program to utopia turned out to be a hoax. Aren't you an immigrant too?"

"No, I'm not an immigrant. My friends and I were brought here after an attempted revolution in Washington."

"Well, a lot happened after the revolutions."

"Really? Tell me about them."

"After the revolutions, everything was actually peaceful on Earth. Honestly, people everywhere were happy. Then these invaders tricked us with a tourist program. We all completely fell for it. We came in our millions to experience a visit to Planet Xanadu like fools. The cities we were taken to were something you could never imagine."

"Their cities?"

"Yes, their cities were magnificent and unimaginable. The technology, the landscape, the beauty, the freedom, the peace—everything was just unbelievable and indescribable, everything was wonderful. In fact, it seemed like heaven, a complete dreamland to us. Then we were offered the chance to immigrate permanently. And from what we had seen during our visits, we thought that it was a great idea. Through the immigration program, they offered us jobs, free healthcare, free housing—and we fell for it in our millions. Millions and millions of us took the bait," the Ugandan sighed. "We were naive and foolish to believe them. And here we are now, taken from Earth and thrown straight into these mines to work for them until the day we die. We are all slaves, my friend."

"No, I think you're wrong. Maybe there's been some mistake? You aren't supposed to be here."

"No, we aren't wrong. We asked and challenged them. And guess what their reply was?"

"I can't say."

"They said that we got exactly what we were promised—jobs for life in the mines, rent-free accommodation in the prison cells, free food and free healthcare as well.

We are slaves of Planet Xanadu, and we're going to work in the mines until the day we die."

Jeffrey gasped. "Slaves? You mean we are all slaves?"

CHAPTER 18

After their rations had been served, the prisoners began to eat. But Jeffrey was barely eating, just picking at his food. He was completely lost in thought as he reflected over what the newcomers from Uganda had told him. Slowly, the realization began to dawn on him. They were telling the truth; every one of them in that prison on Planet Xanadu was a slave.

Jeffrey was still pensively toying with his food when the screens around the hall came to life. There were over twenty of these screens inside the hall and each of them measured at least a hundred inches diagonally. These huge screens displayed images in real-time and exactly to scale, so that they matched real life at that moment. On some of the screens were videos showing people from Earth working in the different sectors of the mines. It was clear that they were worn out and completely exhausted as they dug the hard ground there, sweating and looking dirty and unkempt.

On other screens, Jeffrey and the other prisoners in the hall could see pictures of beautiful cities full of people dancing and cheering. The man from Uganda came to sit at

Jeffrey's table and tapped him on his shoulder. "There, can you see? That's one of the cities we were telling you about."

"Where?"

"Here, on Planet Xanadu."

"What could they be celebrating?" Jeffrey wondered aloud as he turned his attention to the screen. The sound of loud music could be heard blaring from hidden speakers around the streets of the city. There were many people gorgeously dressed in beautiful and colorful flowing gowns. There were men, women, and children in the crowds. They all seemed to be genuinely excited, and didn't restrain themselves as they danced around happily. Then he saw him.

Jeffrey gasped as he stood up. But he quickly caught himself and sat down again.

"What's wrong?" the Ugandan man asked. "You seem to be excited."

"Excited?" Jeffrey repeated, as he glanced at the screen again. "I wish I could say that." He pointed at the screen. "Isn't that Davius?"

"Who?"

"Davius. It's Davius! That man on the screen, the one smiling merrily there," Jeffrey pointed.

Right there, amongst so many people dancing on the streets of the beautiful city, was Davius himself. He was beaming and dancing excitedly to the loud music.

After a while, Jeffrey saw Davius beckon to someone. It was a woman. She hurried over to his side and he whispered something in her ear. She nodded and left, leaving Davius to continue to dance.

A couple of minutes later, the woman returned and whispered something else into Davius' ear. He nodded. Not long afterwards, about twelve men and women appeared. They were dressed in royal regalia with crowns and scepters in their hands. Their gowns were white and very long, to the extent that they were covering their feet and dragging on the floor behind them. On their heads they wore crowns of gold which shone brightly. In their right hands were staffs that measured about four feet long. At the ends of the scepters were round balls that were reminiscent of gold doorknobs back on Earth.

As soon as these newcomers appeared, everyone bowed down low and continued to dance with their heads lowered in reverence.

"Behold, dear citizens of Planet Xanadu," announced a voice over the speakers. "We hereby welcome the exalted presence of our Ruling Council Members." The crowd began to rejoice and cheer as the Council Members walked up and onto an elevated stage, one after the other in a single file. Once they got onto the stage, they all spread out, forming a semi-circle.

One of the Councilors stepped forward. She raised her hand in front of her, as if in salute to the people that were gathered before them.

Once the crowd saw the gesture, they all fell silent. No one was dancing anymore and the music had gone quiet.

Davius was smiling broadly and proudly as the Councilor started to speak. "Fellow citizens of our great Planet Xanadu," she said. "I welcome you all to this grand event on this special day." As she spoke, the camera zoomed in on her, relaying her image to several screens, billboards, and televisions all over Planet Xanadu.

"I'm sure many of you must be wondering why we are celebrating," she continued. "Well, you need not wonder at all. We are all excited and happy because all of our ships that left Earth have successfully returned home to Planet Xanadu. Our mission on Planet Earth has been more than successful; it was a *tremendous* success. We were able to return with over five billion healthy and productive men and women—over five billion free slaves, all of whom are going to be deployed to work in our mines in more than twenty sectors. As you can see, we are all celebrating in the City of Opulence, where the last of the ships has arrived with our new slaves. We invite you all, the free citizens of Planet Xanadu, to join us in our celebrations. Thank you."

The crowd roared and clapped in excitement at her statement. She raised her hand to bring them to silence once more. "This feat of ours would not have been possible had it not been for the hard work, dedication, and coordination of one of the finest officers that this planet has ever been able to boast of. Yes, I am talking about our very own Commander Davius."

At this statement, Davius was spotted by the camera crews and they zoomed in on him to get a closer shot. Davius smiled and waved at the cameras as his image was being beamed all around.

"To show you all just how elated we are by Commander Davius' commitment and hard work on Earth," the Councilor continued. "We are conferring upon Commander Davius the highest military honor—the Medal of Grand Commander of Planet Xanadu."

The crowd began to cheer again as two of the other Councilors stepped forward. Another aide ran up onto the stage, carrying a small box in her hand. As she handed it over to the two Councilors, she bowed her head low.

The first Councilor smiled. "Could Commander Davius please step forward so that we may bestow this honor upon you?"

The crowd was still cheering as Davius walked briskly to the stage. He was waving his hands at the crowd as he made his way through the people around him. Once he got to the stage, he bowed his head to the Council Members.

The two Councilors holding the box beckoned to Davius until he came closer to them. They opened the box and took out a purple medallion on a gold chain. The medallion and the chain were both glittering as the Council Members held them out. They both reached forward towards Davius, who bowed his head as the medallion was placed around his neck.

But the two Councilors were not done yet. They reached into the box again and took out what looked like a brooch. It had a design that comprised two leaves and a feather, with two small rifles crisscrossing each other. They unhooked the pin behind the brooch and attached it onto the front of Davius' grey bodysuit.

Once they were done, the two Council Members stepped back. Davius smiled and straightened his back. He then stood upright with his chest out and his feet together. As he saluted the Council Members, the crowd began to clap and cheer.

The Council Members smiled and began to clap their hands too.

Davius bowed at the Council Members on the stage before turning to face the jubilant crowd. The cameras caught his image as he was waving and smiling around the stage.

Jeffry turned to the man from Uganda. "Did you hear that?"

"Sure. You've heard it from them directly, right? There was never any immigration program; it was just a ploy to trick us to come and work for them."

"I should have known. I should have known!"

"You couldn't have known," said Bradley, who was sitting opposite them at the table. "The Future People were always in charge. They had us and our leaders in the palms of their hands right from the start. We could never have known the truth of their intentions. We could never have known."

The news of Davius' award was being beamed all over Planet Xanadu.

***

In his cell that night, Jeffrey found it difficult to fall asleep. He found himself tossing and turning for hours.

While recalling the celebration, he remembered noticing that he and the other prisoners were working in mines surrounded by massive walls. He shook his head. *No wonder they don't have many armed guards in the mines*, he mused. The prisoners were allowed to move freely without handcuffs, since the walls were wide and high enough to deter anyone from thinking of jumping or climbing over them.

But something struck Jeffrey as he was watching the ceremony on the screens; there were also the same massive walls around the City of Opulence. This meant that the people in Opulence were well-safeguarded and protected. And this knowledge made Jeffrey realize that the cities must not be too far from the mines where he and the other prisoners were working.

Eventually, when the idea of sleep had deserted him, he sat up. He drank a glass of water before lying back down on his bed again. He glanced at his watch. The time was a few minutes past three. He glanced around the cell room. He saw the chair in the corner, as well as the desk. There was a mirror on the wall. In it, he saw a reflection of himself that he didn't like. He looked older than he remembered.

The words of the newcomer resonated in his mind; *they had been given everything they were promised in the immigration program—a job, free accommodation, free food, free healthcare.*

Jeffrey thought about their condition. They did in fact have all of those amenities, for free—but this hadn't been given to them in the form of genuine consideration or entitlement reserved for special people like immigrants.

Jeffrey snorted. *Special people indeed.*

But come to think of it, they actually have everything they need. Everything that a person needs in life is available thanks to the people of Xanadu. They have accommodation and food, and they're being well-taken care of.

The only thing we lack is our freedom. And there is nothing that a living being desires as much as freedom.

Even animals in captivity want to be free, let alone intelligent beings like humans who have been taken away from their homes under false pretenses. Freedom is a right that every human desires and should be entitled to.

But do the people of Planet Xanadu realize this?

Do they understand that freedom is a universal principle? One that should be respected and granted to every living being?

Jeffrey shook his head in disgust. *How could they be so comfortable invading Earth just to take as much manpower as possible to work for them?*

The prisons that Jeffrey and the other slaves lived in were based in the middle of an ocean on a giant island. There were several high-rise well-designed buildings, properly-structured and constructed to accommodate the entire population of Earth if the need arose.

Each prisoner had his or her own room. In each of those rooms, there was a comfortable bed, a desk, and a bathroom. The floors were all paved with expensive marble. There was a touch of luxury in each of the rooms; it felt like being in a four or five-star hotel back on Earth. The rooms didn't feel like prison cells in any way. Prisoners felt like they were living in tastefully-furnished rooms in a big and expensive hotel.

Every morning, cargo shuttles were sent to ferry the prisoners to the mines, which were situated on the mainland. The mines in question were separated from other parts of the mainland by high walls.

This meant that anyone who thought of escaping from the prisons would have to overcome the massive body of water that separated them from the mainland, and anyone who thought of escaping from the mines would have to contend with the massive walls that separated them from the cities.

Jeffrey sighed. He clenched his fists as he reached a decision about what he had to do.

At six in the morning, the alarm went off. It was the wakeup call. Jeffrey didn't need the alarm, since he was already awake.

He joined the other prisoners to file out of the prison facility. As he moved, he kept searching through the crowd until he saw who he was looking for. He moved quickly.

"Bradley," Jeffrey hissed.

Bradley turned, "Jeffrey, how are you?"

"I'm okay. Where is Martins?"

Bradley scanned the crowd, then pointed ahead. "Over there."

Jeffrey followed his finger and nodded when he saw Martins. "I want us all to meet today."

"What are we meeting about?" Bradley asked.

"I'll let you guys know when we meet."

Bradley nodded. "Okay. Where will we meet, in one of the mines or at lunch?"

"Let's meet in one of the mines. You know what to do?"

Bradley nodded. "Sure. We'll make sure that we all work in the same mine. That means getting into the right queue to take us there. Where are you going to be working?"

"I'm going to be in the gold mine in Sector 67TW. Let's all find the queue that will lead us there."

Bradley left to pass on the message to Martins.

Meanwhile, Jeffrey searched for the queue that led to the gold mine in Sector 67TW. Once he found it, he fell in line behind the other prisoners. Just before he climbed down the ladder, he glanced back over his shoulder.

"What are you looking for, 367AD?" asked the armed guard by the stairwell.

Jeffrey smiled back at her. "I'm just wondering if I should be here."

"Wondering? Don't you know where you want to work today?" she asked. He saw her finger wrapping itself around the trigger of her automatic laser rifle.

Jeffrey snapped his finger. "No, I definitely want to be here. Thank you."

As soon as he got into the mine, Jeffrey picked up a shovel and began to dig. Not too long afterwards, Bradley and Martins joined him.

"Fancy setting up a meeting in a gold mine," Bradley said, as he picked up a shovel and joined Jeffrey.

"I had to choose a mine where we could discuss things as quickly as possible," Jeffrey said in a low voice.

"As quickly as possible?" Martins repeated. "What could be so urgent that it couldn't wait for lunchtime or later in the evening?"

Jeffrey looked around before continuing. "Have you noticed that our number has increased massively in the past few weeks?"

"Yes, I noticed, I was wondering what had happened on Earth."

"So, I met some newcomers yesterday."

"Newcomers?" Martins asked, scooping up some sand with his shovel.

"From Africa—Uganda, to be precise."

Martins frowned. "Ugandans? Did they rebel too?"

"No, they were part of the immigration program."

"What immigration program?" Martins asked.

"From what he told me, after we left Earth, the so-called Future People offered the people tourist trips to this planet, and after that they offered an immigration program and people took the bait. Our people immigrated in their millions. All the immigrants were brought here with us to work in the mines. It wasn't an immigration program, but a slavery program. We are all slaves on this planet."

"So it *is* true after all? All that they were saying about their successful mission on Earth, the billions of people that were taken, and how they are now slaves here—that's us? It's all true?" Martins wondered.

"Absolutely true," Jeffrey confirmed.

"That's terrible!" Martins spat. "They're cruel and heartless!"

"Yes, they are all those things and more. But we can't keep reeling off all the bad things about these invaders from Planet Xanadu. I called us here today because I want us to do something about it."

"What do you mean?" Martins asked.

Jeffrey glanced around, trying to see if he could spot any of the guards nearby. There were none. "I want us to break out of here."

"A jailbreak?" Bradley asked.

"Yes, and we're going to take every single human with us."

"That's insane!" Martins said.

"No, it's not insane to want to break free," Jeffrey pointed out. "It would be insane if we refused to do anything to get out of here. Over five billion! Just think about it; five billion of us are on this planet because we were scammed."

"So what's the plan?" Martins asked.

"We start a revolution. I've studied our locations; the prisons are based in the middle of the ocean, so it's impossible to escape from there. The mines, on the other hand, are inland and surrounded by high walls that separate us from the cities—so, that's our best bet."

"I see. So, a jailbreak and a revolution on top of that. Wonderful ideas, I must say. But you're forgetting two critical facts: one is that we are prisoners, and the second is that we don't have any weapons," Bradley said.

"Yes, I've already thought about that. We don't need weapons to fight. We have enough numbers."

"Numbers? What do you mean?" Martins asked.

"We're going to stop working in the mines, then begin to protest and march against them."

"You mean like a strike? You want us to go on strike here in the mines?" Bradley asked.

"Guys, this is insane!" Martins struggled to keep his voice down. "How can we protest against these people? Can't you see those laser weapons of theirs?"

"And can't *you* see that there is strength in numbers? Come on, over five billion of us can cause some major mayhem if we try to."

"Jeffrey is right," Bradley said. "If we are well-coordinated, we can overcome them easily. But that's only if we are well-coordinated."

"Yes, we're going to have to plan carefully in order to succeed. Once that's done, we can transport every one of us back to Earth by stealing their spaceships."

"So, how do we go about organizing everything?" Martins asked.

"Simple, we pass on the message to other prisoners and get them to pass it on to more prisoners, until such time as every human being here is aware of our plans."

"But first we have to pick a day to start the strike," Bradley pointed out.

"And we must also make sure that everyone understands that this is a mission that will set us free from the shackles of these scammers," Jeffrey added.

"Yes, definitely," Martins said. "And the sooner the better."

Jeffrey nodded. "We can spread the message while we eat in the halls, bathe, and even work in the mines. We will be discrete so that the guards and troops never suspect a thing."

"Okay, so when do we start the strike?" Bradley asked.

Jeffrey paused to think. "I'd suggest within the next twenty-four hours."

"Twenty-four!" Martins exclaimed.

Jeffrey quickly hushed him. They continued to dig quietly for a few minutes while glancing around. Luckily, none of the guards had paid any attention to them.

Jeffrey turned back to Martins. "You heard me; twenty-four hours. Tomorrow by this time, we should have started the strike and the revolution."

"But isn't that too soon?" Martins asked.

"The sooner we strike, the better for us. Right now, they are excited and distracted. In this sort of mood, the prison security and other troops will have let down their guard. They will not be so alert because they are busy celebrating their supposed success over Earth. This is the best time to strike."

Bradley nodded. "I agree with Jeffrey. When an enemy is celebrating, they are at their most vulnerable position. If we had known earlier, we could have started today."

"They're still going to be celebrating for the rest of the week," Martins said.

"Are you sure?" Bradley asked.

Martins nodded. "Yes, I overheard some of the prison guards discussing it yesterday."

"Then we have to move fast," Jeffrey added. "We should still strike tomorrow without delay."

"So, what now?" Bradley asked. "We start informing the others?"

Jeffrey nodded. "Later at lunch we can spread the message, or we can even start now. It should be simple and straightforward; everyone needs to be ready for a revolt tomorrow. Once we arrive in the mines, we will strike and refuse to work."

"Then what?" Martins asked.

"We make a move to take control of Planet Xanadu. Once we are successful in overthrowing their Ruling Council Members—we can get our people—and transport everyone back home."

Bradley rubbed his chin. "That's quite ambitious. But if we were to simply get our folks and return back to Earth, don't you think that these invaders might regroup and come after us?"

Jeffrey shook his head. "No, we're not going to leave any room for that to happen. When we have overpowered them, we must make sure that we subdue them and disable them completely. What I'm proposing is that we make this planet a colony of Earth, such that when we eventually make our return back to Earth, a mission could be sent back to Planet Xanadu to come and take over command."

"I like that," Martins said. "We should make them a colony of Earth. They have an abundance of mineral resources like this gold of theirs—we can use it to rebuild everything that was destroyed back on Earth."

"We get to colonize the colonists, invade the invaders, and take control from the Future People!" Bradley grinned. "I like it."

"Yes, but we need to be focused. We will fail miserably if anyone starts revolting back in the prisons—we'd still be trapped on the island, so we have to make sure everyone is in the mines on the mainland to succeed."

Bradley nodded. "You're right about that, Jeffrey. If we overpower the guards here, we can make our way to the City of Opulence more easily. But in the prisons, we don't have any link across the ocean to the mainland."

"Except for their cargo shuttles," Martins pointed out. "The ones that ferry us to the mainland every morning."

"But remember that those are all electronically controlled. If the guards get wind of any altercation or uprising in the prisons, they could easily shut down all the cargo shuttles so that none of us could get to the mainland," Jeffrey said.

Bradley shook his head. "That would short-circuit our plan completely. No, we can't start our campaign from the prisons. We dare not risk being cut off from the mainland."

"Exactly," Jeffrey nodded. "And that's why we must start from the mines. Once we are in the mines, we only need to contend with the walls that surround us, not some huge body of water."

"No problem then," Bradley said. "We'll start right away."

As he watched his generals dispersing to different parts of the mine, Jeffrey continued digging. Soon, he could see them whispering to the other prisoners. Jeffrey smiled. The word was already spreading.

CHAPTER 19

Later at lunch, Jeffrey met with several other prisoners and told them the message. It was simple and straightforward, something that everyone could easily remember: *'Tomorrow, we march from the mines to the walls and our freedom.'*

The message moved quickly. Once Jeffrey informed the first set of prisoners, they in turn informed the others and so the message spread like wildfire. By the evening, when they were all being ferried in the cargo shuttle back to the prisons, every prisoner had heard about the strike and revolt that was planned for the next day. Even though they were in the midst of heavily-armed soldiers, each prisoner had a knowing look as they exchanged furtive glances with each other.

They knew that the next day was going to be their day to freedom.

***

The next day, Jeffrey woke up early. He didn't want anything to appear out of the ordinary, even though he already knew that everything was set to happen just as he and his generals had planned. When it was time for him to leave his cell, he walked cheerfully out of it. He had to resist the urge to begin whistling merrily.

As he joined the prisoners in the queues that led to the loading bays where the cargo shuttles waited to ferry them to the mines, he exchanged knowing glances with the others. He could see a glint of excitement in everyone's eyes as they nodded to him.

Jeffrey saw his generals in separate queues. They also nodded at him, then Bradley made a fist with his left hand, holding it close to his leg. It was a subtle gesture but one that Jeffrey's trained eyes had seen. *'Everything is ready to go as planned'*, Bradley was telling him. Jeffrey made a similar sign by clenching his right fist and holding it close to his right leg. *'We're all ready'*, he was saying to Bradley.

They all successfully boarded the cargo shuttles. Jeffrey held his breath as the first cargo shuttle took off, then the next, and the next, and the next. He could mentally picture all the cargo shuttles taking off one after the other until they were all airborne and heading for the mainland.

As they flew over the ocean, Jeffrey let out a sigh of momentary relief. He knew that the most sensitive part of their plan was making sure that everyone left the island. If they didn't all leave the island prison, then they couldn't completely focus on the mission at hand. It would have been very disconcerting for Jeffrey and the two generals to coordinate their plan on the mainland if they knew there were others left in the prisons.

Luckily, this didn't happen. All the prisoners were safely ferried across the ocean to the mainland. As they flew, Jeffrey took his time to take in the view of the water below. He knew that if everything went according to plan, it would be the last time he would see this ocean. As for the prison, he made a mental note that they would convert it into a museum if they ever came back, something similar to Alcatraz on Earth.

But that's for when we return, Jeffrey reminded himself. *For now, we have to stay focused on the mission on the mainland.*

They soon arrived in the mines. One by one, each of the cargo shuttles landed and the loading ramps were dropped. The armed soldiers directed the prisoners as they all filed out of the shuttles. Once everyone was out of the cargo shuttles, the soldiers instructed the prisoners to choose which mine to work in for the day, by joining the corresponded queue. This was the normal routine.

Jeffrey smiled to himself when this happened. *Perhaps this was one of the rare good points about these invaders. They never forced any prisoner to work in any particular area on any day of the week.* There were several mines for people to work in, including the silver, gold, diamond, and titanium mines. Someone who worked in the silver mine one day would not be under any obligation to work in the same place the next day. All a prisoner had to do was to select where they wanted to work and signify this interest by joining the respective queue.

When they were being directed to select their queues, Jeffrey knew that everything was running perfectly as planned. The soldiers and the guards didn't suspect that anything was amiss. If they had, they wouldn't have asked the prisoners to select their queues. Perhaps they wouldn't have even been ferried from their prisons in the first place.

So far so good. Everything is working according to plan, Jeffrey mused.

The queues of prisoners were gradually growing. Jeffrey was currently standing in line for the gold mine. He glanced at the front and saw that there weren't many people in front of him. Excusing himself, he left his position and quickly moved to the front so that he was the first person in it.

There were four armed guards that were escorting them. As he moved to the front of the queue, one of the guards glanced at Jeffrey. "You, 367AD! Why are you jumping the queue?" she asked.

"I want to get a good spot for my digging today," Jeffrey replied.

The guard chuckled. "That's the spirit, slave! You'd better rush and get some good work done."

Jeffrey glanced at her as they walked. "Slave?"

She grinned. "Yes, 367AD. You are a slave, just like every other person working in the mines."

"But we're only prisoners, we cannot be slaves."

"Think whatever you like, but you'd better realize the truth—you are all slaves."

Jeffrey nodded but didn't say anything else. He glanced around furtively. He caught sight of Bradley, then Martins. They were all at the front of their respective queues, heading for different mines. *Slaves indeed,* Jeffrey thought. *It's only a matter of time now.*

By the time they arrived at the mine, Jeffrey could feel his heart beating with excitement. Since he was at the front of his queue, he would be the first to reach the ladder. But when he got there, he stopped, then turned around and started shouting at the top of his voice, "March!"

"March, march, march!" Jeffrey continued to scream.

The guards cocked their guns and aimed them at Jeffrey.

Suddenly, he raised his right hand high in the air and started running towards the walls.

This was the signal every other prisoner had been waiting for. They all understood what had to be done. Without hesitating, they all turned and put down their work tools.

Once they had done so, all the prisoners charged towards the guards. As they charged, they were all screaming and shouting "March, march, march!" Alarmed, the guards took aim and began to fire their laser rifles.

Some of the prisoners were shot down immediately. It was as if someone had used a very sharp scythe to mow down the stalks of ripe corn in a field. A lot of the prisoners fell down. Others, who were still on their feet, started running back towards the mines to escape the firing.

Bradley quickly scrambled up the ladder. As he did so, he saw the injured prisoners ahead, as well as the ones that were rapidly advancing towards the pit. He could sense the mayhem that was about to ensue; especially the mayhem that he was about to cause.

Spotting one of the guards, Bradley took three long strides until he was upon him. The guard fell face-forward with a scream as Bradley clobbered the guard's head from behind and twisted it sharply to break his neck. Then Bradley stood up and raised one hand up in the air, before he started running and screaming. "To the walls! To the walls!" And suddenly, all the prisoners who were running to escape the guards' wrath turned and started running in the opposite direction, following Bradley and screaming, "To the walls! To the walls!"

CHAPTER 20

All this was happening so quickly.

Jeffrey ran towards the guards, knocking one of them down. He snatched away his laser rifle and opened fire on the guards. Several of them were mown down so easily from such a short distance. The others that tried to take aim at Jeffrey were soon overpowered by the prisoners. Soon, the prisoners were ripping the guards apart. It was as if a pack of wolves had descended on some hapless lambs. It was a complete massacre. Body parts were being ripped off and tossed into the pits with wild abandon.

Soon, word got to the other guards and soldiers in the mines about what was happening. But before they could respond, the prisoners who were with them turned and pounced on them. Reinforcements were mobilized to face and tackle the ensuing mayhem and uprising. But they were too late and too few. The prisoners numbered in their billions. In spite of their laser firearms, they were no match for the sheer size and number of the billions of prisoners from Earth.

Soon, it was over. The prisoners had successfully overpowered all the remaining guards and soldiers, killing quite a few in the process.

The remaining guards who were not killed were rounded up and tied down. They feared for their lives, wondering what was going to happen to them. In such hostile situations where a revolt takes place, anyone that is taken captive would suspect that their lives would be ended. They didn't feel that they were prisoners of war who should be spared; especially not after the way they had mistreated and manhandled some of the prisoners.

With the revolt successfully completed, Jeffrey, Bradley and Martins led the people towards the walls. They were massive, and extremely high. They were the only obstacle that separated the mines from the outside world of Planet Xanadu. The engineers who had designed and built those walls, had done so to keep the prisoners inside. They were tall and formidable. But Jeffrey and his team were determined.

Working together, the prisoners began to form human ladders, climbing one another like acrobats in a circus. Gradually, they had created numerous ladders and soon people were able to reach the top of the walls and climb over.

Once this had been accomplished, those on the top of the wall created another set of human ladders to get themselves down the other side of the wall.

It was while they were at this stage of their campaign that the spaceships started arriving. Jeffrey was alarmed; it was obvious that someone must have alerted the military forces in the City to what had been happening in the mines.

As soon as the prisoners saw the spaceships approaching, they began to panic. But Jeffrey and his two generals were up to the task. They quickly mobilized the prisoners. While some were busy coordinating the climbing over the walls, others gathered the weapons that had been rounded up from the guards and soldiers that had been subdued a while ago. Once their weapons were ready, they began to open fire on the oncoming spaceships.

While the prisoners were firing at them, the spaceships opened fire in return. Some of the human ladders were sabotaged, as people were shot and some were killed. But the prisoners didn't relent in their efforts at crossing over the walls.

Jeffrey and his generals continued their onslaught against the spaceships with the few laser rifles that they had salvaged earlier. Soon, quite a large number had been immobilized and destroyed. For those that crashed, Jeffrey sent some men over to them to salvage their firearms, missiles, and every available form of weaponry that they could find. With these additional weapons, they were able to defend themselves better from the additional reinforcements that were arriving from the City of Opulence.

But even the military forces of Planet Xanadu were found wanting; there were just too many prisoners. The more they fired and attacked, the more they seemed to increase in number. It was an almost impossible task to eradicate all of them. Five billion people was an enormous number. Five billion prisoners who were determined to escape for their lives was an even more daunting prospect. Five billion people with nothing to lose proved impossible to subdue. The soldiers had been firing and shooting at them all the while. A lot of the prisoners had been injured, and many more killed already. But they just kept on increasing in number. How many could they really kill? There were just too many of them.

The severity of the situation became evident when the first group of prisoners successfully climbed over the walls and began to group up to invade the City. Jeffrey and his generals had been able to commandeer some of the spaceships and were using them in their attack on the City.

Once they had regrouped, the prisoners began their march towards the City of Opulence. Overhead, Jeffrey and some other prisoners were flying the spaceships that they had commandeered from the attacking military forces. While they flew, Jeffrey spotted some more oncoming spaceships. Because the spaceships were not aware that the oncoming ships had already been commandeered, they felt that it was safe, and continued to fly towards the mines. That was when Jeffrey and the other generals fired upon the other spaceships, shooting them down from the skies before they could even understand what was going on.

The few that did avoid the onslaught, couldn't escape Jeffrey and his generals' coordinated attacks. Soon, the remaining reinforcement spaceships were cornered and they faced one of two choices; either they accepted defeat and surrendered or they took the risk of fighting back. They took the lesser of both choices and gave in, surrendering to Jeffrey and his generals.

Now with additional spaceships in their fleet, Jeffrey had even more firepower than before, when they had begun the initial campaign at the mines. Back then, they had struggled against the guards and soldiers, collecting minimal firepower, including laser rifles and other ammunition. Now, they were better armed with more than just laser rifles.

They now possessed superior aerial firepower in the form of advanced spaceships. Now, all that remained for them was to head for the City of Opulence and take over the government.

CHAPTER 21

"We've done it!" Bradley cried out. "We've overpowered the invaders. We've done it!"

"No, not yet."

"Not yet?" Martins repeated. "But Jeffrey, we've defeated them already. We have!"

Jeffrey frowned and said nothing. He glanced outside. They were all inside one of the spaceships that they had just commandeered from the military forces that had been sent to quell their uprising in the mines. From where he stood on the bridge of the spaceship, he could clearly see the ground below. It was a tarred road with white markings. Since the road was so clear, it was almost as if they were driving on the road inside a normal vehicle, but they weren't. Rather, they were inside a spaceship that was hovering and flying a few feet above the ground. On both sides, Jeffrey could see other spaceships flying along with him. All of them were maintaining the same altitude, almost hugging the road underneath them, while flying at a moderate speed.

There was an important reason for them to maintain such a low altitude—they were trying their best to avoid being detected. Jeffrey and his generals knew that the City of Opulence must have some kind of motion detection and surveillance systems. They didn't want to alert those systems.

Another reason was that they wanted their compatriots on foot below to be able to catch up with them. Jeffrey wanted to strike the City of Opulence with everything they had—and now they had a lot. Forget were the few laser rifles they had scavenged from the guards and soldiers in the mines; now they were in possession of sophisticated spaceships with heavy firepower. But beyond all the stolen ammunitions and firearms, Jeffrey knew that they possessed something else which was far more important—the element of surprise.

He knew that as long as they could continue to sneak up on the City the way they had planned, they would be able to overpower the defense systems and guards with minimal resistance and relative ease.

The City of Opulence had sent a fleet of spaceships some time ago to check up on the mines and quell any sort of uprising that had been taking place. The people of Planet Xanadu had confidence in their machines, soldiers, and systems. The wall that surrounded the mines was gigantic, tall, and formidable. Their soldiers were dedicated and very experienced. Their firepower, spaceships, and ammunition were both impressive and superior. There was simply no way a group of prisoners would be able to overpower the arsenal that had been deployed to the mines.

But that was where the people of Planet Xanadu had got it wrong. Jeffrey and his fellow compatriots weren't just ordinary prisoners. They were prisoners who had determination and a single focus. They also numbered over five billion. Five billion determined and focused people who wanted to be liberated. Nothing could stop such an uprising and revolution. Simply nothing.

"Or haven't we?"

Jeffrey blinked and turned to look at Martins. He shook his head. "No, not yet. We haven't. We still have the City to take over. All we've done so far is subdue their first line of defense. But with the element of surprise on our side, we will surely succeed in crushing their main base—the City of Opulence."

Both Bradley and Martins nodded. "Yes, you're right," Bradley offered. "The City of Opulence is the big target. That's the main prize."

"And that's our destination," Jeffrey added. "As long as we stay at this speed and don't trip up any sort of alarm, we will be on them in no time."

"What do you think their state of readiness will be like?" Bradley asked.

"State of readiness or state of preparedness?" Jeffrey asked. He reached forward and tapped on the panel before him. The widescreen in the spaceship came to life—they were watching a live feed of activities within the high walls of the City of Opulence.

Nothing in the live feed seemed to be out of the ordinary. People could be seen moving around peacefully and happily. Others were enjoying their leisure time in what appeared to be amusement parks and recreation grounds. Small hover vehicles were moving around, flying at low altitudes to and from their various destinations.

Jeffrey scanned the images. He adjusted the angles of the feeds and scanned further reaches within the walls.

Apart from a handful of armed men and women strolling around casually, there were no groups of soldiers anywhere.

"Nothing," Jeffrey confirmed, satisfied.

"Nothing?" Bradley repeated.

Jeffrey shook his head. "You can see for yourself. There's nothing. They aren't expecting us at all."

"Funny, isn't it?" Martins wondered. "You would think that after sending out their spaceships to check up on their mines, they would have taken measures to protect themselves by beefing up security there. But they haven't."

"They seriously underestimated the resolve and the willpower of five billion prisoners who were desperate for freedom," Jeffrey said.

They continued to fly slowly, as the walls of the City of Opulence loomed far ahead. Soon, they were within two hundred yards of the perimeter fencing. Jeffrey turned to his generals. "This is it," he said. "We should all get ready to hit them with maximum force and firepower."

Bradley and Martins nodded. They turned on their systems and communicated with the fleet of spaceships under their command.

By now, the walls were clearly visible. They seemed to rise up out of the ground and tower straight up into the skies.

"They are even taller than I anticipated," Jeffrey observed.

Bradley nodded. "Far taller. They are even taller than the ones at the mines."

"Foolish people!" Martins spat. "They think that these high walls will protect them from the resolve of the people who have been abducted from their homes and turned into prisoners? Into slaves?"

"Well, they are about to get the shock of their lives," Jeffrey said. "With these spaceships, we will get over the walls and open their gates for our people. Quickly, tell them to rush to the gates!"

Bradley and Martins nodded and began to communicate with the ground crew, while Jeffrey contacted the other spaceships. Their plan was simple: those that were flying the spaceships would head over the walls and immobilize any personnel and systems that were manning the gates. Once this had been done and their ground troops had gained access to the City of Opulence, they would search and destroy any military machinery and attack the people of Planet Xanadu within the walls.

On the ground, the prisoners had received their latest instructions. They immediately set to work, heading for the enormous gates that manned the city.

The gatekeepers and guards on duty were still in a joyous mood because of the celebrations that were taking place within the City of Opulence. Some of them were drinking, while others were chatting excitedly. Unlike other days, none of them were particularly focused on what was happening at the gates or on the access roads leading up to them.

One of the security guards lifted his bottle of beer and took a long sip. As he did this, he caught sight of the empty road that lead to the gates. It was empty. *Of course, it should be empty,* he reasoned as he lowered the bottle. They generally didn't expect anyone to be on the roads, since most citizens usually preferred to fly personal hovercrafts instead of travelling by road. It was only in rare situations that some citizens might decide to go on a road trip, but those were very rare. He turned to chat with his colleagues, then raised the bottle to his lips again. As he lowered the bottle the second time, he gasped and almost choked.

His colleagues at the security post frowned when they saw him choking and pointing. They glanced at each other, wondering perhaps he was simply joking or trying to make fun of them. After all, everyone was celebrating. But the guard in question didn't stop. Rather, he continued to point and cough. When he saw that no one was responding, he reached forward and grabbed the shoulder of the closest colleague to him.

The security guard that he had grabbed was shocked—but before he could react, the first security guard had turned his head, and was using the beer bottle to point at the other side of the wall. The second security guard frowned, but then his eyes widened in horror and disbelief.

The road that was supposed to be empty was now full of people; not just any people, but the prisoners from the mines, armed with laser rifles and other weaponry.

The security guards at the post immediately dropped their drinks and scrambled to reach for their weapons and controls. In their scramble, one of them ran to the post and slammed his hand on a big red button.

"They cannot get in! No matter what!" he cried out. "I have activated the automatic lockdown on the gates."

As missiles were fired towards the gates, they just blew up on impact without leaving any visible damage. No matter how many more missiles the prisoners fired, they just kept exploding without achieving anything. The missiles had no impact whatsoever because the gates were made out of extremely strong, advanced materials.

Realizing this, the uprising began to focus their attention on the walls—but the missiles couldn't make a dent in those either. Both the gates and the walls were impenetrable to the prisoners' missile attacks.

From where he was in the spaceship at that moment, Jeffrey could see that some of the spaceships had broken away from the main fleet. They were flying speedily towards different parts of the walls. Alarmed, he turned to Martins and Bradley. "What's wrong with those spaceships? Where do they think they are going? Tell them to maintain formation. They need to maintain formation!"

Martins began to reel out the instructions over his intercom, but Bradley shook his head and turned to Jeffrey. "It's too late."

"What do you mean it's too late?" Jeffrey fired back. "Call off those guys now! Where are they going?"

"Can't you see?" Bradley asked, pointing at the spaceships that were heading for the walls. "They're on a suicide mission. They're going to ram the walls."

Jeffrey stood up. "Suicide what? No, no, no, stop them! Stop them!"

But it was too late. They all watched in horror as the spaceships rammed straight into different portions of the walls, exploding and creating large clouds of fire, smoke, and debris that scattered all around.

Jeffrey was shaken. He shook his head in disbelief as he slowly sank back into his seat. "They didn't have to," he said slowly.

"Well, they just did," Bradley confirmed. "And in the process, the integrity of those walls have been severely compromised. Look, they're now crumbling and falling apart in several places!"

They looked more closely at the walls and saw that it was true. In several places, the walls were already coming down, collapsing in a heap, paving the way for the ground troops to enter the city.

Jeffrey sighed. He couldn't have imagined that any of the prisoners who had been piloting the spaceships would have gone to that extent just to create access points for the ground troops. As he watched the walls continue to collapse and crumble in several places, he recalled the fall of the Berlin Wall back on Earth a long time ago. But this wasn't the Berlin Wall; this was the walls around the City of Opulence.

Jeffrey sighed again. He shivered as he thought of how much the will-power, focus, and determination of a group of people could drive them to overthrow and overcome any dictatorship or government in power anywhere—whether back home on Earth or right there on Planet Xanadu.

The security guards had also seen the walls falling down in several places. The laser fire from the spaceships was now more effective. The prisoners' attack was targeted and focused, easily disabling the mechanisms that controlled the towering gates—so much so, that the gates were now swinging wide open on their own.

The security guards realized what had happened, but it was too late. Their defense systems were compromised and the gates were broken, giving unfettered access to a rampaging mob of armed and angry prisoners. There was nothing they could do other than to run.

As some guards started to run away, others felt the need to take a final stand, and picked up their weapons. Taking aim, they began to fire at the prisoners who were already spilling into the city through the gates and the walls. They were like millions of ants infiltrating an enemy colony. Initially, the prisoners were intent on getting deep into the city—but with the fire coming from the security posts, they had to take cover and return fire.

The security guards were no match for the firepower of both the ground troops and the spaceships above.

Suddenly, some other spaceships began to break away from the fleet. "What now?" Jeffrey asked. "What are they doing?"

Martins looked up from his console. "Don't worry, I just got confirmation from them. They're going to pick some of our fellow prisoners and ferry them into the city to speed up our attack."

"I see," Jeffrey nodded, feeling more relaxed.

Soon, more of the spaceships were landing and picking up the prisoners who were still far outside the walls. They would then take off and ferry them into the city before returning for more.

Jeffrey had already seen the exchange of gunfire between their fellow prisoners and the security guards on the ground. He turned and pointed below. "Get some of our spaceships to provide cover to our people down there," Jeffrey said to Bradley and Martins. "Some of the security guards are making a stand instead of running away."

Martins and Bradley communicated the instructions to the other spaceships. Jeffrey saw three of them veer away and head down towards the security posts. As they approached, they began to attack with advanced laser weaponry. One by one, each of the security posts was reduced to a pile of burning and smoking rubble.

"Great, great, great!" Jeffrey cheered as he saw the success of the aerial onslaught. "Now we'd better proceed quickly into the city. Make sure that we subdue each and every armed soldier they have."

CHAPTER 22

Davius was drinking and smiling to himself. He was in his office, sitting behind his desk with both feet on the table. He was still dressed in his uniform. He was holding the brooch that he had been awarded by the Council of Elders. He took another sip from his glass and smiled to himself. He knew he had gained the confidence of the Council. He couldn't wait for his next assignment.

Perhaps they would consider sending me to explore a new planet in a different solar system. I just can't wait to go on another mission. He smiled again and took another sip.

Then he heard the first boom. It was very loud and very clear. It was also very close, because it made several items in his office shake and rattle. Then another one sounded, followed by another, until the explosions were happening in rapid succession like gunfire. And with each explosion, more items in his office began to rattle loudly.

Davius knew that it couldn't be gunfire. No one dared fire a gun in the City of Opulence.

When he heard another series of booms, he swung his feet off the table and ran to the window to look outside. Not too far from where his office was located, he could see several enormous clouds of black smoke. It was as if several people in the city had decided to light giant bonfires. The clouds of smoke were so thick and dark that the skies were quickly turning black, as if they had been painted over.

Then he saw the spaceships—several of them flying ahead, releasing heavy laser fire on the city.

Davius cursed. *How could my people—my very own soldiers—be firing within the City of Opulence?*

But he had no time to consider an answer. From his office window, he could see several residents running for safety as the first wave of prisoners gained access to the main streets. They were firing laser rifles and other weapons at random.

Davius cursed when he recognized the prisoners. He didn't bother processing how or why they were in the City of Opulence, a place that was well separated from the mines where the prisoners were supposed to be working. He could only understand that, somehow, they had succeeded in commandeering the spaceships, which was why the city's own weapons were now being used against them.

Davius dashed to his table and pulled open his drawer. He took out a laser pistol and checked the cartridge to make sure that it was properly loaded. Satisfied that it was, he ran back to the window and surveyed the scene once more. He caught sight of three prisoners shooting a laser canon at some houses. Davius swore under his breath as he slid open his window. He took aim and fired three shots from his laser pistol. The three prisoners went down immediately. As they fell, their fellow prisoners were taken aback and tried to determine where the shots had come from. By then, Davius had already ducked down so they couldn't see him.

In the meantime, Jeffrey was encircling the area from above. He could see the big clouds of black smoke rising up from various locations in the city. It was their handiwork that had led to this damage. And it was just the beginning.

He caught sight of smaller spaceships flying out of a hangar down below. Jeffrey veered off course and followed them. The smaller spaceships were no match for the size, speed, or sophistication of the gigantic ones that Jeffrey and his generals had commandeered. Once he had the new spaceships in his line of vision, Jeffrey opened fire immediately. One by one, they were blown to bits as Jeffrey's laser firepower cut through them like a hot knife through butter.

Then, Jeffrey directed their ship to the hangar where the small ships had come from. He directed their laser canons to shoot at the building, and peeled away just as it went up in an enormous explosion.

By now, there was chaos everywhere on the ground. The once serene and beautiful City of Opulence was now overtaken with confusion, disorder, and destruction. Everywhere anyone turned, there was rapid laser gunfire, mortar blasts, and explosions. Clouds of smoke could be seen rising from several buildings, while citizens were running around aimlessly, screaming and looking distraught and confused. Others were crying, unable to understand what was going on.

Jeffrey checked the map logs on board the spaceship. There was someone he had to get in order to be completely sure that the war was going to be decisively won in their favor: Davius.

Jeffrey knew that until Davius was either caught or killed, they were still at risk. He wasn't concerned about the Council Members, just Davius—because after all, it wasn't the Council that had invaded Earth in the first place. It was their stooge, 'Commander Davius'.

Jeffrey looked up from the monitor he was studying. "Bradley, Martins, we need to get down there as fast as possible!"

"Down there?" Martins repeated. "But the ground troops are doing a good job already."

"No, I'm not suggesting that we should assist the ground troops," Jeffrey pointed out. "I want us to find and apprehend Davius."

"Of course!" Bradley cried.

"From these digital maps here, I've been able to pinpoint his office. I'm now using the city's monitoring system to track him down to wherever he is at this moment. Once we zero in on exactly where he is, we have to get down and apprehend him."

"Agreed," Bradley said. "And what about the Council? What should be done to the Council Members?"

"We should deploy some units to their chambers and ensure that they're all rounded up and tied down, just like we did with the guards and soldiers at the mines," Jeffrey said.

"I'm on it," Martins nodded, before picking up his intercom and passing on the instructions.

"Now we zero in on Davius," Jeffrey said, peering at his monitor.

Meanwhile, Davius was still in his office. He was taking shots at the prisoners down below, killing quite a few of them, while injuring and maiming several others.

Jeffrey cross-referenced the ship's database and monitoring systems, then discovered that someone was shooting at the prisoners from a building assigned to the highest ranks of Planet Xanadu's military. He smiled.

"Quickly!" Jeffrey called out. "Let's head for that building. I have a hunch that Davius might be there. He could be the one causing us so much damage from that spot."

Davius was still shooting from his office window when he saw the huge spaceship zoom down onto the street in front of him. As soon as he saw it, he realized that he had been tracked down.

As Davius ran out of his office, Jeffrey directed his laser missiles.

As soon as the missiles hit their mark, the entire building was obliterated and reduced to nothing but smoldering rubble.

Jeffrey checked his scanners for movement. The scanners then paired with the monitoring systems in the area, catching sight of someone running from the back of the building. Jeffrey enhanced the images, and the identification systems alerted Jeffrey that it was Davius.

"It's him!" Jeffrey jumped to his feet. "That awful bastard is still very much alive!"

"What do we do now?" Bradley asked.

"He's trying to get away," Martins said, pointing at the screen.

They could see Davius moving through the backstreets, avoiding the mayhem and laser gunfight that was going on around him.

"He doesn't know that we're tracking him," Jeffrey said. "Let's deploy a few people to track him using the coordinates we have here."

Bradley got in touch with a regiment of prisoners on the ground. "We are going to relay you his exact position from our servers on board this spaceship," Bradley said. "Make sure you approach him with all the firepower you have. And when you do, make sure that he is apprehended."

From their spaceship, Jeffrey, Bradley and Martins watched as thirty or so prisoners broke from their attack formation and rushed to the backstreets. Using the directions relayed to their communication devices, they were able to track Davius to the exact spot where he was hiding. When they were within a hundred yards from him, they split into three units to surround him.

At that same moment, Davius was already making his way through another backstreet. He could hear the sound of sporadic laser gunfire. This was punctuated by the louder, more vicious sounds of laser cannon fire, heavy laser artillery, and bomb blasts all around. The sounds of chaos, mayhem, and confusion were accentuated by the sounds of people crying, screaming, and calling for help. Davius shook his head. He couldn't imagine how the once peaceful and serene streets of the City of Opulence had suddenly degenerated into such a war zone. Everything had happened so quickly, without any warning or anticipation.

How could all this have happened? Davius wondered as he ducked behind a flower garden and peered out. Ahead of him was an open and empty street. There was no one in sight.

He shook his head. Moments ago they were celebrating the success of their campaign on Planet Earth, but now everything had descended into this—a full-blown war of gigantic proportions.

Davius held his forehead. He couldn't think straight. *What's going to happen to the Council of Elders now? And the people of Planet Xanadu? There's only one way to find out,* Davius said to himself as he stood up and crept out of hiding cautiously. He had to get to the City Centre where the Council of Elders was always in residence.

As he started to move, he heard a rustle from his left. He paused, ducked down, and peered in that direction. The visibility there was poor because of the smoke, but he could make out the movement of human shapes. There were several of them.

He didn't stand up again. Rather, he turned to crawl towards his right. As he did, he saw a flash of light. He froze. Something was wrong, he thought. This wasn't an ordinary flash of light. It was the reflection of light from a firearm—a laser rifle.

Now Davius knew what was happening. *Somehow, someone has spotted me. If I take either of the routes to the left or right, I will surely be caught.*

I have to get out of here at all costs!

Davius checked his laser pistol, then dialed it to maximum power and paused. He peered at the empty street in front of him.

He knew he had to make a run for it; he had to make a run for it before whoever was trailing him from his left and right could catch up with him.

With his arm outstretched and the laser pistol in front of him, he stood up abruptly and began to run. As he did so, he could hear shouting all around. He didn't pause to see the prisoners coming out from both directions with their guns blazing. He just ran ahead, swiftly taking aim and hitting the prisoners on both sides. As he ran, several of them fell to his expert marksmanship. They were also firing, but they couldn't get a direct hit.

Davius kept on running and shooting. All of a sudden, he had to stop in his tracks. Right there in front of him, on the street that he had thought was empty, was another group of prisoners charging at him. Confused, he turned to his left and then his right. There were more prisoners coming from both directions, heading towards him.

Dropping to one knee, he began to fire on and on, shooting and maiming quite a number of prisoners in the process. As they opened fire on him, he somersaulted, rolled, and landed on his feet, dodging several laser gunshots in the process. He rolled again and found himself behind a hedge. He scanned the area, weighing up his options. He had to move quickly or else he would soon be surrounded.

But just as he was about to make a move, a giant shadow fell over him. He didn't have to look up to know that it was one of their spaceships.

"Put down your weapon, Davius," said a voice over the broadcast system. "Put down your weapon and no harm will come to you."

Jeffrey was on board the spaceship that was now hovering over Davius. He could see Davius peer upwards with his laser pistol still in his hand.

"I know what you're thinking, Davius. But if I were you, I would comply with the instructions. Put down your weapon and surrender peacefully," Jeffrey added.

Davius slowly stood up. The laser pistol was still firmly in his grip as he got to his feet. By now, the prisoners who had been tracking him had made a circle around him. Davius looked at them, then glanced up at the spaceship.

Then, without warning, he dropped to his knees and took aim at the spaceship above. But Jeffrey had already anticipated his move. Before Davius could take a shot, Jeffrey had already released a laser gunshot. Davius screamed as his right hand was severed. He stared in horror as his hand fell to the ground, still holding onto the laser pistol.

A metallic ramp slid down from the hovering spaceship and Jeffrey used it to walk down from the craft. He walked up to the injured Davius and bent down to look at him. "I warned you not to make a move, didn't I?"

Davius was bleeding and shivering. "You won't get away with this!"

Jeffrey smiled. "You think so? Well, that's where you're mistaken." Jeffrey turned to the prisoners nearby. "Tie him up well, and take him to join the others."

CHAPTER 23

Davius was sitting on the ground. All that was left of his right hand was a stump, enclosed in a bloodied bandage. The prisoners were all around him, armed with laser pistols and other light weaponry. He glanced up and saw spaceships hovering around. Clouds of smoke were still billowing from nearby buildings. The roar of heavy gunfire could be heard, punctuated by the screams of people in the distance.

Jeffrey nudged Davius' shoulder with his rifle. Davius grimaced and looked up at him. "I'm not going to ask you again, Davius," Jeffrey said. "How do we get into the Sanctuary?"

Davius shuddered involuntarily, still clutching his bandaged hand. "I can't tell you that. I can't."

Jeffrey pointed the nozzle of his laser rifle at the stump of Davius's arm. "You've already lost a hand. Are you willing to lose more because you refuse to cooperate?"

"I can't. You have to understand that," Davius pleaded.

Jeffrey shook his head in disdain. "Now, you listen to me, Davius. What I understand is that the Sanctuary is where your Council is—and my men and I need to gain access if we want to capture them alive. Once that is done, then we can be sure that Earth will never be invaded again. Since you are their most trusted General, you can help us get in."

"I can't tell you. Please, I can't!"

"Okay. I see." Jeffrey turned to some of the prisoners as he adjusted the settings on his rifle. "Hold out his left arm for me."

Davius shot a glance at Jeffrey as two of the men held him tightly, while another held out his left arm. "Wait. What is this? What are you trying to do?"

"Trying?" Jeffrey repeated. "I'm not *trying* to do anything. I'm about to do something—amputate your left hand."

"But you can't do that! That's barbaric and inhumane!"

"Is it? That's funny. Did you not think of those concepts when you were invading and decimating Earth?"

"We were fair to you all!"

"Fair? I don't remember you being fair. But that's a subject for another day. Right now, I will do what has to be done, which is to detach your left hand from your body."

"Okay, okay, okay! I'll tell you what you need to know."

Jeffrey lowered his laser rifle. "Okay, go on. How do we get into the Sanctuary?"

"You already know where the Sanctuary is."

"Please, don't start that with me now," Jeffrey cut him short. "Yes, we already know where the Sanctuary is. All we want to know is how to get in."

"The Sanctuary can only be opened from the inside," Davius said.

"Yes, I think my colleagues and I have already figured that out. But of course, none of the Council Members are going to do that, seeing that there's a revolution taking place in their city. How else can we get in?"

"I can let you in," Davius said.

Jeffrey shook his head and sighed. He raised the laser rifle again. "Are you going to get to the point or what?"

"Yes, yes! The main entrance to the Sanctuary can be accessed from outside by anyone who has been given prior clearance and authorization."

"And by anyone, I'm sure you are referring to someone like you?"

"Yes. And a select few others."

"And how do you do that? How do you get into the Sanctuary?"

"The Sanctuary's systems will authenticate my biometric information and match it with its records."

"Biometric information?"

"My voice, my handprint, a scan of my retina, and a scan of my face."

"Ingenious," Jeffrey said. "Is that all?"

"I must use the correct pass code as well."

"Pass code? What's the pass code?"

"When I get there I will say it."

Martins stepped forward. "What does he mean when he gets there? Why doesn't he want to tell us now?"

Bradley held Martins by the shoulder. "Calm down, Martins. Even if he told us what it was, it would be completely useless to us because it would only work with his biometrics, not anyone else's."

"Yes, Bradley is right about that. Just calm down, Martins. We'll all go to the Sanctuary together. Let's see how this works," Jeffrey said.

A short while later, their spaceship landed outside the enormous structure housing the Sanctuary. It was a dome-shape with three towers. It reminded Jeffrey of one of those cathedrals that had been built during the medieval times on

Earth, except that it was completely sealed. The walls were smooth and shone like something made of gold, silver, or another precious metal. The edges of its walls were coated with ornamental jewels and stones. There were no doors or windows anywhere.

Jeffrey turned to Davius, who was being held behind them. "Well, go ahead," he urged. "Open the Sanctuary."

Davius nodded and stepped forward. He placed his left hand on a part of the wall, then looked directly at it. As he did this, he blinked several times.

Jeffrey and the others saw a beam of red light come out of a small hole in the wall. The beam of light fell on Davius' face and began to scan his facial features. After a while, the light disappeared.

"Biometric information for Commander Davius confirmed," said an electronic voice. "Speak clearly for your voice to be recognized."

Davius cleared his throat. "Commander Davius."

"Voice recognition for Commander Davius confirmed," said the electronic voice. "What is your mission at the Sanctuary?"

"I'm here to see the Council of Elders."

"What is the pass code?"

"The people of Earth are our slaves."

Martins gasped. "The people of Earth are what?"

Jeffrey and Bradley motioned to him to keep quiet while they all waited.

After a few seconds, the same electronic voice spoke once more. "Pass code for Commander Davius confirmed. You may now have access into the Sanctuary."

A section of the wall began to slide upwards into the rest of the building. As it did, an entrance was revealed to them all. It was the size of a standard door and was illuminated with bright light.

Davius turned to Jeffrey. "We'd better go in now. The door closes in exactly sixty seconds."

Jeffrey nodded and signaled to Martins, Bradley and a handful of other people from Earth. He asked the others to remain stationed outside the entrance while they went inside to confront the Council Members.

Once the last of them had entered, the section of the wall slid back down, cutting them off from their colleagues outside.

"Did he just say that 'The people of Earth are our slaves' was the pass code?" Martins asked again.

Jeffrey nodded as he looked around. "He did. Do you have a problem with that?"

"Do I have a problem?" Martins repeated. "They are so arrogant, so derogatory! It's disgusting."

Jeffrey shrugged. "Well, they were invading us. So they came up with something that suited their egos and twisted minds." He turned to Davius. "What now? Where are they?"

Davius pointed up ahead. "They will still be in the main Chamber."

"Doing what?"

"Celebrating."

Jeffrey frowned. "Celebrating? While the rest of the City of Opulence gets leveled?"

"That's how this Sanctuary was designed. It was supposed to shield the Councilors from whatever was happening in the outside world. They will only know when they are updated."

Bradley stepped forward. "Wait. Are you trying to say that they still don't know about our escape from the mines, or even the revolution taking place right now?"

"No, they won't know. They will only find out when they are briefed of the situation on Planet Xanadu. Their briefings are every three days. The last one was yesterday, so they are not expecting to hear anything until two days from today."

"And they're comfortable with things like that? I mean, not knowing what's happening in real time?" Martins asked.

"They've always let things run that way. They don't like being disturbed with day-to-day or administrative issues. They trust that my colleagues and I are capable of handling things on their behalf."

"Madness!" Martins hissed. "Complete and utter madness! What kind of false leadership style is that?"

"Calm down, Martins," Jeffrey said. "We are not here to judge their ways, remember? We are here to apprehend them." He turned to Davius. "Alright, lead the way."

Davius led them down the path until they came to a corridor, where he pointed to a huge door. "They will be inside that chamber."

"Celebrating?" Jeffrey asked as he glanced at the door.

"Absolutely. They are still celebrating the victory of our planet in enslaving so many of you."

Jeffrey checked the settings of his laser rifle and adjusted it to rapid response attack.

Bradley held his hand. "Wait, what are you doing, Jeffrey? Didn't you say the plan was to apprehend the Councilors? Why are you setting your laser rifle to attack?"

Jeffrey smiled. "Just in case we run into any obstacles inside."

Bradley turned to Davius. "Will there be any opposition inside?"

"None whatsoever."

"You don't mean it? Are you serious? No opposition or guards or security detail of any kind?" Jeffrey asked.

"You still don't get it, do you? Did you meet any security or guards when we were coming into the Sanctuary? Have you seen anyone since we got inside? I am telling you the truth; this place is strictly for the Councilors to relax and have their fun. There is nothing inside that chamber that can stop you from doing what you want to do to them."

"There's only one way to find out," Jeffrey turned to Bradley, Martins, and the other prisoners. "We go in together."

They all nodded. Jeffrey turned to Davius. "And you're coming with us as well."

"Do I have a choice?"

"You already know the answer, don't you? No, you don't."

Once they got inside, they found all the Councilors dancing to some strange music. In most of their hands were champagne bottles that they had taken from Earth. Some were laughing hysterically while others were rolling on the floor with careless abandon. There were trays of food, fruit, and vegetables littered all around—on the tables, chairs, and even on the same floor on which they were dancing. The entire chamber was a mess, and the Councilors who were there completed the perfect picture of ridicule and debauchery.

This was the scene that greeted Jeffrey and the others as they barged into the chamber with their laser weapons pointing ahead.

The Councilors didn't stop whatever it was that they had been doing before Jeffrey's intrusion. Those that were dancing continued to dance, those that were drinking continued to drink, while those that were rolling on the floor also continued to do so. Everyone was completely oblivious of the presence of the armed prisoners.

Jeffrey lowered his laser rifle and turned to Davius. "So these are the people that you are serving?"

Davius shook his head. "Were."

Jeffrey frowned. "Were?"

Davius nodded as he spat on the polished marble floor. "Yes, 'were.' I was serving them, but not anymore. I can't believe that they can descend into such levels of debauchery and shame. Just look at them. They're busy enjoying themselves while our Planet Xanadu is burning to the ground!"

Jeffrey turned to look at the scene again. "Well, that's how you all handled things. But we're here now, and we're taking over completely." He turned to Bradley, Martins, and the others. "Alright, you know what to do—tie them up properly."

As they proceeded to work, Jeffrey continued to watch the Councilors. None of them resisted as the prisoners tied them up. They were too drunk to resist. Most of them didn't even understand who the prisoners were or what they were doing in the chamber of Planet Xanadu's revered Sanctuary.

CHAPTER 24

"Isn't it ironic?" Martins asked.

Jeffrey looked at him. "What's ironic?" They were now outside the Sanctuary with the other prisoners. Davius and the entire Council of Elders were all tied up and kneeling down in a line.

Martins pointed around. "Look, everything that's happening is ironic? We failed to pull off our revolution on Earth. But then we came here and have now managed to overthrow them."

Jeffrey glanced around. He could see their spaceships hovering close by. A lot of the soldiers were still armed with the weapons they had salvaged from the military forces of Planet Xanadu.

Jeffrey smiled and nodded. "Yes, I guess it is."

"So, what now?" Bradley asked.

"We head back home, of course," Jeffrey said. He looked at the sea of prisoners who were standing around him. "I'm sure that we must have some really good fighter pilots from all the nations of our Planet Earth, mustn't we?"

Some men and women began to raise their hands. There were people from China, Russia, France, and so many other countries. Jeffrey nodded. "That's good. You are all going to help fly us back to Earth."

"How are we going to transport this many people back?" Martins asked.

"We will take their spaceships, of course," Jeffrey said. "It's not as if we came here in our own ships in the first place."

They began to board the spaceships. Jeffrey could see that many of them were excited. *Excited and relieved,* he mused.

Soon, the ships were all packed full. Jeffrey gave the signal and they began to take off one after the other. Once they were airborne, he settled down in the cockpit of the mothership. He glanced out the windows as they departed the planet.

It didn't take them long to get to the portal that would lead them back towards Earth. When Jeffrey's ship went through, the others followed behind.

CHAPTER 25

President Parker was drinking tea in her office when she noticed that the room had become darker all of a sudden.

She frowned and looked outside the window. Just a little while ago, it had been a very sunny day outside with bright, clear blue skies. But now the whole place had fallen dark, as if a humungous grey cloud had suddenly come over the White House and its immediate surroundings.

She glanced outside the window for a second time and froze when she saw the spaceships hovering and flying through the airspace above the White House. They must have been in their thousands, and they were all moving and flying around.

When she saw them, she gasped. The teacup fell out of her hand and clattered noisily on the floor as it broke into pieces, spilling tea all over the tiled floor.

"My goodness gracious!" President Parker gasped. "Not again, not again!"

The spaceships were of different sizes. Some were small, others were medium-sized, while others were absolutely massive. But they all were similar in shape and design to the ones that the Future People had first arrived in. Now, they were all boldly entering the airspace and atmosphere above Washington once more.

Is this happening again? she wondered.

Are they back again?

Are the Future People back again?

President Parker shook her head.

I don't believe this is happening. I know this can't be happening, but I don't understand!

President Parker held the side of her table as she felt her heart begin to pound. *This nightmare can't be happening again,* she thought. *The Future People can't be returning so soon.*

Outside the White House, a lot of people had started to gather on the streets nearby. They were all gazing and pointing at the spaceships that had littered the skies, circling and flying around like thousands of birds searching for something of interest down below. Still, there were other people who didn't want to be tempted by curiosity. They had chosen instead to run back to their homes or nearby shelters.

Soon, the police arrived and tried to calm down everyone. They were telling people to remain calm and return to their homes.

But even the police knew that what they were asking for was going to be difficult, if not impossible to do. How could they ask people to remain calm when their skies were filled with the ominous sign of a disaster that had occurred on Earth not too long ago, one that had plunged their entire planet into a state of despair and confusion; one in which over five billion of their fellow human beings had been abducted and taken to another planet far away?

Some police officers were creating a barricade, trying to prevent more people from coming too close to the streets.

One of the officers glanced upwards and pointed. His colleagues followed his gaze up towards the sky.

One of the gigantic spaceships had separated from the fleet and was heading towards the White House. It landed majestically on the well-cut green lawn. A door slid open, then a ramp appeared and extended towards the grass.

Both the police officers and the people who had refused to go home watched with baited breath as they waited for Commander Davius to appear.

President Parker had left her office and was now outside on the lawn. She stood there watching the empty gangway, apprehensive, along with every other person waiting for someone to alight from the vessel.

Then he did.

It was Jeffrey who walked out of the spaceship, with a wide grin on his tired face. As soon as he descended, he walked up to where President Parker was standing still staring at him in disbelief. When he was a few feet from her, he stopped and stood at attention. He raised his right hand and saluted her smartly.

"Madam President, this is Jeffrey Watson, the Defense Secretary of the United States of America. I'm here with the people of our dear Planet Earth. We've returned home."

"Welcome home," President Jane Parker smiled and saluted him back.

THE END.

ABOUT THE AUTHOR

Lamees Alhassar is a prolific, inspirational writer, artist & a philanthropist. You can visit her website http://www.lameesonline.com

More books by Lamees Alhassar

Planet Robani 1
Planet Dan-X34
Planet Nivrus
Planet Pingdingdong
Planet Mandar
Masterpieces The Best Science Fiction Short Stories Book 1
Masterpieces The Best Science Fiction Short Stories Book 2
Masterpieces The Best Science Fiction Short Stories Book 3
10 Paranormal Stories Vol.1
10 Paranormal Stories Vol.2
10 Paranormal Stories Vol.3
10 Paranormal Stories Vol.3
The Magician
The Paradox
Hush – Bad Witch Rising
The Power of Gratitude
How Gratitude Can Give You More

CPSIA information can be obtained
at www.ICGtesting.com
Printed in the USA
LVHW040834160621
690356LV00004B/335